THE SIMPLE TRUTH

BOOKS BY ELIZABETH HARDWICK

The Ghostly Lover
The Simple Truth
A View of My Own: Essays on Literature and Society
Selected Letters of William James (Editor)
Seduction and Betrayal: Women and Literature
Sleepless Nights

THE SIMPLE TRUTH

ELIZABETH HARDWICK

THE ECCO PRESS

NEW YORK

Copyright © 1955 by Elizabeth Hardwick
All rights reserved
First Published by The Ecco Press in 1982
18 West 30th Street, New York, N.Y. 10001
Published by arrangement with
Harcourt Brace Jovanovich, Inc.

Published simultaneously in Canada by
George J. McLeod, Ltd., Toronto
Printed in the United States of America

The Ecco Press logo by Ahmed Yacoubi

Library of Congress Cataloging in Publication Data

Hardwick, Elizabeth.
The simple truth.

I. Title.
PS3515.A5672S5   1982   813'.52   81-43389
ISBN 0-912946-98-9
ISBN 0-912946-99-7 (pbk.)

To my mother, Mary Ramsey Hardwick

THE SIMPLE TRUTH

Early on a cold morning in February Joseph Parks arrived at the county courthouse, an adequate stone structure he had hardly noticed before but which now interested him enormously. Standing in the cold, the courthouse stone turned as yellow as an autumn leaf when the rays of an uncertain sun played over it, or then again under the clouds it would appear merely gray. Parks had the idea nothing was so important as his presence here this morning and apparently others had the same notion of the urgency of the occasion, since a sizable group of spectators had already collected. Among the crowd, those who had come in pairs were the most comfortable and the solitary ones made a great play at appearing purposeful, necessary to the scene that was to follow. Somehow by a bit of coughing and the carefully framed seriousness of their expressions they hoped to deny their motive, which was curiosity.

Joseph Parks was a large young man of twenty-eight whose spirit was lively battlefield where fat and nerve contended endlessly. His face was broad, lighted usually by a cozy smile which revealed his strong, square white teeth. His hair was thick, brown, and healthy, and he had a broad expanse of white-shirted chest. The masculine

pomposity of his outlines and the unqualified friendliness of his face made him appear very much like an old-
fashioned politician, a young man of an old school. Even
in a crowd Parks's bulky affability had a reassuring prominence, not lessened by the nervous quickness of his eyes
which betrayed the considerable affliction he endured: his
desire to articulate his opinions everywhere and to everyone. This need for projection and statement plagued him
like a fever—Parks was immensely friendly, immensely forward. Observant and generous, nevertheless disinclination upon the part of a listener hurt seriously and so the
young man had frequent moments of distress in which he
felt his outgoingness frustrated rather than his sense of
power, as might have been the case with another person
of this bent. As a rule, however, the optimistic fat soon
won out over the hesitant nerves and with a faithful hom-
ing instinct Parks answered objections by a grinning return
to his previous assertion. Most people liked Parks, although
there were some retiring creatures who reacted with flight
before this large, smiling presence, this amiable weight in
the path, this welcoming spirit who never missed a chance
for a greeting or a comment upon the weather. It pleased
Parks, who wore no hat to be lifted, to nod his head pleasantly and without call in the direction of an absolute
stranger.

At the courthouse he eyed the guards, the secretaries,
the sheriff, even stepped very briefly out of his place in the
line to get a peek into the office of the clerk of the court.
He simply wanted to know what these persons looked like,
to add to his store of impressions, and even the sound of
the typewriter, the rouge on the cheek of an aging stenog-

rapher would interest him. "Must be near the retirement age," he would think. "I suppose it's sixty-five in this state too, although I don't imagine the pensions are anything special." In the offices, work appeared to be going on as usual. One man still had his hat on his head and looked as if he had not had time for a sufficient amount of breakfast coffee. But Parks had no doubt that some effort went into maintaining this undisturbed appearance, for this was not a usual morning. Certainly everyone, even the woman nearing retirement, was fascinated and therefore ashamed, as if it were part of a good man's duty to be more placid than usual when something extraordinary and awful touched his life. Parks himself would have denied that curiosity played the major role in getting him out of the house this cold morning. And, in truth, his emotion was so great mere curiosity could not fully account for it.

Hardly looking at the woman standing next to him, he prepared to investigate the possibilities for dialogue. He intended to say forthrightly, exposing his hand as it were, "It puts you in your place when you consider that all this might happen to anyone, any of us here in fact. It certainly makes you stop and think," or in some way to indicate his own position and to learn that of his neighbor.

Parks did not succeed in firing this opening shot because his companion said suddenly, "There he is! Mercy, there he is! At least I believe that's him!" This woman put her hand over her mouth, muffling her excitement.

"Rudy!" Parks whispered under his breath. He was not personally acquainted with Rudolph Peck, a regrettable fact, and yet he often felt he knew no one better. Perhaps he could not claim absolutely certain knowledge of the boy's character because his information was drawn only from speculation, pure meditation. Still, as a mystic is certain of things unseen, so Parks had his own dark ecstasy of the truths beyond knowing.

Rudy Peck had descended upon Parks's sensibility with a tremendous crash, all the force of a dogma, a moral principle embodied in suffering flesh. Indeed Parks felt that, with great advantage to both, he and the prisoner now entering the courthouse lobby might have spent hours conversing about the miserable position in which the latter found himself. Briefly their eyes met and Parks had only the time to stare back vaguely, which was vexing because he desperately wanted Rudy to know he was "all for him."

"He looks better than he did before, not so nervous," someone said about Rudy. But most of the spectators allowed themselves only the shortest glance and then looked into the distance, not wishing to gaze too boldly at the object of their curiosity, their sympathy, or their horror, whatever the young man was to them.

Poor Rudy Peck was a public figure of immeasurable local interest at the moment, of statewide prominence, and of considerable importance to the Chicago newspapers which, with bold headlines and placards, announced they were "covering" him completely. This personable college boy who was walking stiffly through the crowd, wearing a well-pressed pair of gray trousers, a tan tweed jacket, and black knit tie, whose black shoes shone with new polish, whose cheeks were slightly flushed, this boy who had got such a number of people out of bed early was in less than half an hour to go on trial for first-degree murder.

He had from the depths of horror soared into notoriety—all his decent obscurity rising with him, disappearing like a fog, gone forever. Yes, he looked almost as he had before, somewhat paler perhaps, but before his arrest he had not been so much looked at as he wandered about the campus, turned up as a waiter in the local restaurants, went to sports matches, attended his fraternity functions —one more "decent, honest college boy," as the newspapers liked to have it.

"Yes, there he is!" Parks said again to himself. Rudy, the unimaginable, fantastically intact, looking now at his wrist watch, still the ordinary, thoughtful, quite expected college boy, fearfully accused by death, his own actions and statements. Well, he must go through with it, Parks admitted mournfully, almost surprised that this actual being still lived, still conducted himself as a man, shining his shoes, knotting his tie, going up the lobby stairway with some of his old vigor, all his habits supporting him. Parks heard change rattling in Rudy's pocket, noting this with a fascinated shame which he did not know how to judge. Those nickels and dimes—more than anything else that consoling jingling proclaimed Rudy to be a person like any other. And yet he was not. For a moment the unhappy young man stood in the doorway of the clerk's office, as if he hesitated to proceed. Soon his lawyers appeared and Rudy shook their hands with scared magnificence. This group of lawyers and assistants, this "legal battery," circled about him, enclosing him in their warmth, their professional duty, their promising slaps on the back.

"His parents! Look, look there!" someone whispered as this bashful couple made their way through the spectators,

13

their faces painful to behold, trembling, grieved, pitiful, and terrible.

"Ah, I feel more sorry for them than anyone!" a young woman exclaimed.

The wind outside had dampened Mr. Peck's spectacles and he stopped, blushing and coughing, to clean them, while his wife looked on impatiently, as if she were not sure it made a good impression to be cleaning one's glasses at such a time.

"What a pity, what a pity," a man in the crowd observed.

"They seem to be decent people. No reason to look down upon them," Parks said, intending general application and not addressing himself to anyone in particular.

"Who's looking down on them? I feel more sorry for them than *anyone*, as I just told you," an incredibly menacing woman replied to Parks. He decided he would not sit by *her* in the courtroom, and just then the old bailiff opened the swinging doors of the jury room and quietly the crowd entered, each one looking cautious and obedient, careful citizens under the eyes of a traffic cop. Tired of waiting, the people allowed themselves as much hurry as they dared in finding a good seat.

Parks had not made a choice as to where he wanted this trial to take place, but he was not at all satisfied with its having to be decided in Iowa, as it was. The state seemed to him insufficiently subtle for the role it must assume. Of course, Parks hardly knew Iowa, having only recently arrived as a student at the State University. He had even begun to doubt he would ever know this place, the very uniqueness of the state seeming to him to lie in just this impossibility of definition, this way it had of not being what one expected nor yet anything exceptionally original either. Sitting in the middle of the country, Parks found the place an anonymous creation, the work of many singular spirits never quite shaped into a style.

The Iowa weather was candid; the winter was cold, the summer was hot, spring was short and briefly leafy, and autumn slow to arrive. The inland steam-bath summers, during which the corn ripened and promised money for the farmers, struck new townspeople like a plague. They lived through this sweaty eternity, gasping, complaining, and dreaming of lakes and oceansides which seemed a continent away, the breezes and waters of a foreign land. There was always a great deal of interesting talk about the weather in Iowa—and here at least it was a true subject. The relentless gravity of the winters had a certain grandeur, especially when contemplated from inside a house. Outside one was reminded immediately that this was merely the reality of winter, not an esthetic gratuity, because the earth was always difficult underfoot, either as slick as a mirror or as slushy and muddy as a mining camp. Cold, but no grand northern snow sparkled in the winter sunshine, no frozen dry air nipped the cheeks as in Scandinavian tales—wind, slush, slippery highways over which loaded trucks, growling and straining like prehistoric beasts, prowled day and night, snow dripping in a melancholy rain from the trees and roofs.

When a trip to the mailbox in winter requires patience, practice, and a stoical acceptance of nature's discourtesy, a gift for abstract thought is necessary to keep in mind

15

the beauty of things, the sweetness of a patch of flowers rising up suddenly in the dusty air, the brilliance of the gleam of the golden dome of the former statehouse. The older residents had some talents for this, which caused them to speak with exceptional pride of the green grass and budding branch, as if they were unique products of the state. It was not difficult to imagine the citizens of Iowa shared the qualities of the weather: plain, open, their life was not luxurious but not poor either, indeed prosperous; everything was indifferent to the eye and nothing eccentric. The absence of striking excess was a frequent topic for speculation among those inclined in that way. Leading the nation in farm income, where are the lovely, roomy, Iowa farmhouses, they would ask, passing rich acreage with new barns, silos, and orange tractors surrounding a house of cramped, neglected modesty, sometimes pasted over with an imitation brick finish which made it look like a fabrication for the back stage, not for a close view. Baffled, where then are the Grant Wood faces, noble tillers of the Iowa soil? "Retired! Moved to California!" would be the reply.

In this particular Iowa town, the "home" of the State University, most of the transients from other regions were not given to speculation, finding the answer to Iowa difficult to come upon in any case, but simply abhorred the place with a manic volubility. The aliens who had settled for good had more troubled minds, recalling sometimes with a sigh the lost hills and bays of San Francisco, horseback riding in Arizona, and most of all the great East from the Green at Concord to the steak and fish houses of Baltimore—all that glorious, glimmering intensity as of an old

16

capital of an empire, with stone generals in the parks, sedate and glamorous colleges, pictures in the galleries, and wine in the fowl pot. In Iowa a few Southerners even longed for a black face around Woolworth's on a Saturday night.

"It's not so bad when you get used to it," these settlers would say hopefully, but the very necessity of taking up the subject of settling in Iowa brought a charming look of sorrow into their eyes, as if they feared they had been forgotten by dear friends far away. Iowa's unconscionable distance from New York City or Boston, even Chicago, was admitted by these resettled intellectuals, but if the new person did not find that distance unforgivable a list of attractions was tentatively proffered, although hardly ever with the truest confidence, an understandable hesitation when a measure of embarrassment even attaches itself to the sound of the name of the state. Here also at the University were many teachers from Europe, from Vienna, Berlin, Paris, and Madrid, remarkable souls pacing the Iowa pavements, carrying in their pockets a month old copy of *Figaro Littéraire*. They were in America, no doubt about that, even if perhaps they had not bargained for so completely the real thing and wondered at their fate.

The true natives of Iowa, the farmers and the townspeople who sold them insurance, Buicks, false teeth, and Florsheim shoes, did not suffer these spiritual shivers. They liked the name of their state and were not disposed to think up witty remarks about the excellent corn crop. This was theirs and they were of it, blood and bone, educated and formed here like a geological stratum, clear and unambiguous as the crisp, pleasant Iowa accent, which to most ears was hard to distinguish from that of its neighboring states, being of the whole Middle West, the core of the apple.

Twelve of these Iowans were filing into the jury box, taking their assigned places with deep consciousness of the importance of the case revealed in every gesture, and most of all in the churchy thoughtfulness which fell upon them, perhaps for want of any other face to present to the room on this first day. They did not appear happy to be where they were, but still they were evidently there seriously. Joseph Parks, who came from a suburban town near New York City, did not know what to make of them—he knew not a single fact about any member of the jury. They were certainly of "the town," not the University, and therefore he was alarmed, already imagining hostility in one, indolence in another, dry puritanism in a third. They were eight men and four women. The average age of the group had been estimated by the newspapers to be in the fifties, although this mean was not easily visible. The old seemed so very old—a few of them farmers used to doing as they pleased and continuing so, with sleepy nods, toothless smiles, and moving jaws, politely, surreptitiously chewing, as all the while they watched the judge and the activity about the bench with earnest glances. The mobility of the old farmers' faces told no more than the still features, painfully shy, of the other jurors. The brimless hats of the women were friendly, as if the democratic duty to which they were called demanded they like royalty expose their full countenance to the public view. Like the figures in a Dutch painting, the jurors were utterly of this world, breathing and magically familiar, and yet one might look forever without discovering their secret. The latter obdurate fact moved Parks almost to tears.

The law assumed the secret was that the jurors knew nothing, did not read the press with significant care, failed to experience the usual shock at the announcement of a sudden and violent death, lived indeed in a suspension of judgment and feeling, a pure state without opinion which awaited the demonstrations of ultimate truth. No matter that Rudy had been in jail for nearly two months, Betty Jane Henderson was dead and no one in town had talked of anything else. Parks, musing, told himself it was a bit trite to be thinking of these matters, but still concluded they made things "a little less than fair in these law cases." As this necessary assumption of the jury's innocence of attitude was in the manner of a work of art elaborately repeated by the judge—a thing true without being fact—all the twelve faces were inexpressibly attentive and even had a strange, inward beauty.

Sitting just below the jury, Mrs. Peck, the mother of the accused boy, held up her chin with a red hand and Mr. Peck simply sat, a paternal image of profound uselessness for the occasion.

Rudy's mother was large without being fat, with jutting shoulder bones and wide, bony hips, all her frame ample in structure from her head down to her feet, which were large and yet gave the impression of an almost painful narrowness in her sensible black shoes. She had graying blonde hair caught up in a thin bun, pinkish, freckled, dry skin, and fine blue eyes. But the whole of her impression was not to be seized, because she looked at one moment like a tall woman meant to be heavy, who was perhaps indeed heavy, and at another thin, worn down by life. Even her fine blue eyes would sometimes seem to turn as light and dry as her skin. Parks was studying Rudy's parents, tracking their secret hearts, or wishing to. With Rudy's mother he did not know whether to accept the fire of her flushed cheekbone or the ice of her graying blondeness.

Mr. Peck was older than his wife, a sturdy-bodied, brown-eyed working man, a little past the age for tragedy, or so his tired, distracted face seemed to report. He had lived out nearly all of his life, worked hard, and the horror which had fallen upon him came down like a new ache in the joints, stabbing but blurred somewhat by the other, older aches which accompanied it.

There was great excitement on this opening day of the trial, but the case had no sooner begun than many people revealed themselves impatient for the testimony and excitement promised further along the way. Almost immediately Parks's knowledge of dramatic possibility was disappointed; the routine, the busyness, the gradual settling into legal procedure had a clumsy inappropriateness, more suitable he thought to a quarrel over a smashed fender. Parks's sensibilities were real and acute, and at the convening of the court he experienced a feeling of lost opportunity, as if he were the director of an advanced, realistic foreign film of the kind he greatly admired. With half-serious objectivity, he thought he himself might have done better for the prosecution, which was an act of generosity on his part because his bias for the defense was complete. This spectator, Parks, had become as intimate as possible with the case and intimacy, unfortunately, made him well aware of the many difficulties for Rudy, in fact just about every difficulty imaginable in the eyes of the law. Parks's concern was not to deny Rudy's dreadful involvement, but he hoped, or rather *demanded* in his heart, that the jury would see it *his* way, at the same time that he admitted the near impossibility of their doing so. The unlikeliness of these twelve Iowans seeing things in the "right" way was a large part of Parks's own sight, for one can build a philosophy upon the foundation of other people's assumed disagreement. Greedy to help and influence, being unable to reach the jury, pass the time of day, drop a hint here and there, was as distressing to Parks as hunger. He was a savior cut off from his audience.

Catching a glimpse of Rudy's straight-nosed profile when the boy turned to whisper to his lawyer, Parks decided, "He is again as he was before all this happened," giving expression to his powerful wish that somehow nothing *had* happened.

Mr. Garr, the prosecutor, was in his opening plunge no great shakes at sustained address. An appealing if not an exciting man, he put his case before the jury in a halting manner, whether from reluctance or overconfidence no one could guess. Mr. Garr cleared his throat a number of times, spoke seriously, but occasionally a number of syllables in a word banged together and came forth as one. It was an unpleasant duty, this man implied, but nevertheless he was the elected guardian of consequences. Representing the State of Iowa, he was bound to present the facts. They were not so very complicated after all, his direct, simple manner indicated; they were merely dreadful. The State's belief was, he said, that Rudy Peck had not only committed a murder but had done so deliberately and was therefore to be tried for murder in the first degree. It was made clear that the State had not arrived at this charge without thought and study, that it would not present the jury with the charge of premeditation, the desire to kill, without good evidence to support it.

"That's impossible! You can't *prove* that!" Parks thought wildly, as if he had somehow scored a point.

Two months ago on a Friday night in December, Rudy had dashed out of his rooming house at nearly one o'clock in the morning. It was a cold, icy night and almost everyone was in bed except the more sociable students. Lights still burned in the fraternity and sorority houses where parties and dances were held on week-end nights. Slightly drunk, very much frightened and confused, Rudy ran to the police station and told them, "A girl's passed out. . . . Get a doctor . . . first aid. . . . Do something!" and ran back home again, after giving the address. The police, followed shortly by a doctor, and later by a coroner and ultimately by an FBI criminal investigator, went to Rudy's rooming house, a nonofficial residence for men, from which girls were excluded at all times by University regulations.

The rooming house was a shabby-looking establishment, but the ugliness of it was simply another of the incongruities of a region which separated appearance and morality with an evangelical rigor. Actually the house, with its bleak porch and grimy infirmity, was not a scandal nor a charity for the indigent blind as it seemed, but perfectly usual and respectable and accommodated quite a

22

number of respectable and usual college boys, who lived there comfortably enough. It was unjust that this house, with so many seedy kin around it, should have been the one to appear in the newspapers when many others were also excellently designed to tease the irony of crime reporters, just unwashed, public, and neglected enough to call forth the idea of a "secret midnight rendezvous." Crime reporters love their little jokes and cannot resist describing the meanest rural shack as a "quiet love nest." Perhaps they are right to remember "love" even in the most squalid setting, since very few murders are committed because of dirty windows and unraked leaves.

The reporters did not miss their chance with Rudy's rooming house. Isolated from its reassuring setting, the library and University buildings around the corner, it appeared on the inside pages of the press, a clearly criminal-looking place which gave local pride a jolt for a day or so. Study lamps and books seemed out of place in it. It was, however, exposed to the public eye in its essence, a very plausible scene for a murder and might have been standing there waiting to achieve its function.

These houses, as rakishly unkempt as a band of outlaws, rented rooms to students and teachers and were said to be the expression of an idea even more than of landlord greed. They were the local revenge, retribution for the accusation on every student's lips that the "town would be nothing without the University." The town had the notion of maintaining its identity by being *nothing* even with the large school and thousands of students squatting unhappily in it.

Suitable to the extraordinary prosperity of the section,

there were, in addition to the official dormitories, new houses for students—the hybrid, costly suburban mansions of the student fraternities and sororities, buildings that aspired to the exclusive and grand. Some of these inventions were said to have cost as much as ninety thousand dollars and even that sum did not satisfy apparently, because the façades were miracles of bizarre eclecticism and camouflage meant to suggest an infinitude of building dollars. Huge white columns supported a stoop no wider than a newspaper; perilous balconies decorated great slabs of red brick; Tudor castles hinted at all sorts of interesting nooks and crannies within and pieces of dull pink glass suggested a cathedral theme here and there. These houses, recognized by their Greek letters twinkling in colored lights, were like gypsy palaces. Sometimes one could see the girls' stockings and underwear hanging on the line or a plaintive third story without window curtains—these lapses humanized the structures even if they did not quite justify the singular combination of public function and hominess which was embarrassing to the sophisticated, of which Parks was one in this respect, or enthralling to others—to Rudy himself, no doubt.

It was, indeed, possible to draw grim moral instruction from the bare house in which the death occurred, but even here the fluid, democratic mysteriousness of Iowa surpassed everything: to live in the ugly rooming houses did not at all establish that one was a penniless student. It did happen that Rudy's parents lived in modest circumstances and that his father was a "worker," and yet the son too belonged to a social fraternity and the year before had lived in one of the mansions, sharing a bright room dec-

24

orated with sailcloth and dining at the fraternal board. It also happened that his parents were in their early years immigrants from Finland, and no doubt some of the citizens of Iowa liked to think of these newcomers as queer and poky. So to that degree Rudy came from a victimized group. And yet he was a popular, outstanding boy with an air about him which, far from suggesting a foreign country and a tormented peasant class seeking opportunity, did not even suggest Iowa, his birthplace, but rather the East. He might have been a student at Yale or Princeton.

When the police arrived at the rooming house after midnight on that Friday, they found Rudy's room in a flood of light, and on the bed the body of a beautiful college girl, Betty Jane Henderson. It did not take long to establish that she was dead. While the boy sobbed and moaned, "Do something! For God's sake, help her!" the police stared wonderingly at the lovely girl whose golden slippers were visible beneath the hem of her dress of striped taffeta. She lay as if wrapped in a ceremonial scarf, brown and golden and red as October hills. Beside her on the bed, touching her arm, lay her fur coat. "What sort of business is this!" a policeman said softly, nearing the bedside.

The doctor arrived shortly, confirmed the death, and noted the bruises on the girl's throat and several deep puncture wounds which looked as if they had been made by fingernails. Clumping up the steps, sleepy and astonished servants pursuing their awful report, came the coroner, the photographers, the newspapermen. Outside the room, the other boys who lived in the house stood together, frowning and silent. And in the terrible room

25

itself, Rudy, slumped in a corner, almost unnoticed, kept begging for some miraculous intervention or, despairing that, he cried out the desire to die himself. "I'm done for. . . . I don't want to live . . . not another minute, not one! Kill me now instead of later!"

Getting up from the chair, he touched a policeman's arm. "Will you?"

"Will I what?"

"Shoot me!"

"No."

And suddenly, coming abruptly to life, the men who had been called out in the cold night began to work rapidly and the scene came to an end as bewilderingly as it had begun. The body was carried away; Rudy was given his overcoat and escorted to the police station. In what seemed just a moment, the room was dark, locked tight, and the baffled and shivering boys who had gathered in the hall went now to their own rooms to talk throughout the night.

For Rudy the night passed and the morning came on without sleep. Hour by hour his behavior changed as he sat with the police and county officials. The whisky, never a great amount, wore off quickly and he said now that he and Betty Jane Henderson had been in his room earlier in the evening, when he had prepared a little dinner for her before going to a dance given by his fraternity. Yes, he knew she was not allowed in his room, he admitted wearily. And then after the dance they had come back for a nightcap. He said he and Betty Jane had only been joking, and in play he put his fingers on her throat—and after that he remembered nothing. Five or so blank, frightened minutes during which she was dying before he went to the police station for help. Surrounded by the law, alone, he asked for some moral or spiritual comfort for himself. What did he want? Hesitating, this young man of his time said he would like to see the faculty psychologist and through this request it became known he had seen the psychologist before, some months earlier. Why? For various reasons, he said, but the newspapers discovered with no difficulty that he had sought an explanation for impulses of self-destruction and ambivalent feelings about the girl he loved, Betty Jane Henderson.

On that next morning, Joseph Parks awakened to the desolating newspaper account of Betty Jane Henderson's death. Stepping gingerly out on the porch to snatch the paper, Parks discovered that immense things had been going on while he slept. "How strange! Who are these people? Right here in town, too!" he said aloud, although he was the only person awake in the three-story house. Large and robust as he was, Parks had the sort of insomnia which did not allow him to sleep late in the morning, even if it did not usually prevent him from dropping off immediately at night. When the sun came up, Parks came up with it. The rays called to him through carefully lowered blinds, as if delivering him a special message. Because of this early rising he often felt he was suffering, as some say of the sun itself, a gradual loss of heat and energy. What was worse—as a student in Iowa, Parks hadn't the proper setting for this compulsive coming awake at six o'clock. Sometimes he longed for a flower garden to gaze at from the window, as he had seen his father do in the early summer mornings, or for a kitchen downstairs where he could brew his solitary coffee and fry bacon like an old cowhand in the dawn. Occasionally, he even dreamed of baronial acres and himself, genially middle-aged, surveying the dew on the grass. But these were merely dreams, leaving him the moment he was fully awake. Only the old cowhand at his two-burner stove seemed a decent wish for a young man who was skeptical of privilege.

Parks tiptoed upstairs with his newspaper, a large, friendly, crumpled figure in a moth-eaten, plaid woolen bathrobe which he prized dearly. Carefully he settled himself into a corner of the living room, into an unscreened square which the landlady had described as, "your kitchen . . . Very compact and practical, don't you think?" Here in a space no bigger than a broom closet a little one-story icebox was topped by a stove and bounded on the left by a small sink.

Parks's wife, Doris, had turned over into the spot vacated by her husband's early rise from their double bed, which was in another corner of this same one-room apartment. Although only of moderate size this single room had so many recesses given over to some function of housekeeping usually placed alone that there was hardly anything, unless it might be the little spot in the center covered with a tiny, red tufted rug, that could properly be called the living room itself. Books sat on the floor and blue crockery plates rested in a narrow bookcase; the toaster used the same electric plug as the phonograph; Rouault's clown dangled from a large nail and a clay African god, made by a student friend, lay this morning with his head in the bread basket. Passage in and out of the door was slowed down by the nearness of the rail upon which this young couple's clothes hung. The apartment was rather like a dwarf's dressing room in a film studio, but

29

unfortunately both Parks and his wife were of normal growth.

Neither the young man nor his bride, Doris, was accustomed to this bruising compactness. They were black and blue from turning these swift corners and making their way from the sharp edge of the table to the sharp edge of another table used as a desk. Their long legs strode over their domain with a few steps, sometimes crushing some of their bright possessions underfoot. Yet, despite the blows and knocks, they were both still sleek and clear-eyed from the enormous comforts of their childhood; they were liberal, careless and amused rather than irritated and might have been on an archaeological tour instead of "setting up housekeeping." Doris's father was a lawyer and Parks's was a doctor. They both had lived in Larchmont, New York, from which, each day, their fathers went by train to their offices in New York City.

Parks and Doris were living in Iowa on the GI Bill, supplemented by occasional checks for a hundred dollars from their parents. Of course, Joseph had already been to college before the war and was now seeking further preparation for life. They had come to this from the protection of their middle-class families, those families very properly called "comfortable" who provided an atmosphere of even heat in the winter, a month at the beach in the summer, good cuts of beef at all times, two bathrooms, and education in private schools. Doris and Joseph, like most of their contemporaries, were no sooner married than they fell, as if it were a pit beneath the altar, into a life thoroughly disorderly, unhandy, and always short of cash. It was all fun and not the least bit frightening to them, even if nature did seem to be working out a mysterious plan by giving one more money at the age of twelve than one had as a husband with the rent coming due. Nothing had so much told them they were really married as the disappearance of all they were used to, that prodigal world of light and cleanliness, two-car garages, rumpus rooms in the basement, polished furniture bought in Connecticut antique shops, mountains of clean linen in cedar-lined closets. All of it was gone; it might just as well have vanished in the 1929 crash before they were old enough to care.

Parks imagined the pinch of chagrin he sometimes felt about his present lodgings came only from the dishonest cost of the rent, but still at such times dear, old objects, clean and roomy, soft and sunny, would come into his memory: his green-and-white striped chair at home, his reading lamp and little table, just the right size and height for a pencil, ash tray, a plate of grapes and apples, his "study" lined with books and his desk—memorable, unbelievable object from a golden age—his desk, nearly as large as the square called their kitchen! He did not truly remember these things as something he longed to have again and certainly not with resentment. They simply returned to his mind, releasing him for the moment from a generalized sensation of muscular restriction and the frequent dizziness that came over him, especially when he had spent some time fruitlessly searching for a letter carefully saved. In this little flat to save anything was to bury it until one was packing up again for a move. Very few things were worth the trouble of excavation.

Still there was a certain charm in this rattiness. Not

everyone was capable of it, this couple seemed to think. And certainly the most inexperienced person would have known the moment he set foot in the apartment that it was not the home of the hard-working poor. It was much too messy for that. Silver dishes and table settings tarnished in the cabinet, evening dresses and a suit of tails gathered dust on the railing, expensive luggage was stacked in the hall. Waste and poverty jostled each other on the friendliest terms, without one being absolutely sure where necessity lay.

Doris Parks had rather a lively mind, which did not help her much with the housekeeping but enabled her to arrive at a few general principles about the very core of the problem. She did not for a moment accept domestic duties as *given,* but had the idea that many were easily avoidable if only one had the proper attitude toward these chores, if they were accorded their place and no more. This young wife had what she called a "moral abhorrence" of excessive, nervous housekeeping and saw a nearly mad "Craig's wife" where others would have seen only a reasonably steady cleaner. Doris found the sink and the bathtub turned gray without a good deal of scrubbing and even what she considered a "good deal of scrubbing" —a few turns with the water spray and a bit of mopping up with a cloth—was not always effective. Remembering white sinks all her life, she admitted further measures must be called for, but she was reluctant to investigate these fully, having a contempt for all the new cleansers and detergents. "I'm bored with all these new products," she would say, laughing. "Why, you could spend all your time just keeping up with the names!"

32

"Just get one and stick to it," her husband advised.

"But it isn't so easy to remember which one is mine," Doris would say.

She discovered that the dishes from their meager breakfast, the plates for the cold luncheon sandwiches, the glasses for the milk, the pot for the coffee, took an alarming amount of time, which somehow ought to be spent more profitably, and so she arrived at the radical solution of doing the dishes only once a day, after dinner. Doris remained faithful to this economy even though there were seldom enough dishes for dinner. But that was not so great a difficulty as the powerful promptings to conformity represented by the Iowa housewives on the two floors below them.

"I saw her at the clothesline again today," Doris would whisper, looking out of the window. "Just yesterday too, this same one, not the woman on the first floor! And then there's the ironing. It's too much to think of, the poor things. They even iron the sheets and *I think*, if you haven't got servants, you ought to put them on without pressing. They smell so outdoorsy too, that way. . . . It's probably healthier."

Doris was, these days, spending as much time puzzling over the way to be both a housewife and a "free person" as she had only a year ago in college struggled with the complexities of disarmament. "Baking breads and cakes with icing dotted with red candies! How sad it makes me, Joe. And the number of pans all this takes. You see, they start out, these women, with everything spick and span, the kitchen *absolutely perfect* and they dirty it up all over again in the afternoon for the cake! And then they wash

33

all *that* up, before they start getting everything dirty again to cook dinner! Now this is not just once in a while, but every day—if it's not a cake, it's cookies or rolls or some dessert made in the afternoon and also the ironing, the cleaning, the baby—and you know they even wash the woodwork *quite* frequently! I've seen it. The other morning that nice girl on the first floor . . . up a ladder washing the bathroom ceiling! Looking as tired as a dog, too, really worn out."

Doris was sincerely moved to pity for the other women in the house, young, amiable Iowa wives with children. Sometimes she felt her own spirits dampened by the swishing of the sponge floor mops below or the noise of the vacuum cleaner. When she saw one of her neighbors waxing the steps of the common stairway, she almost wept. "You shouldn't do that," she said tenderly. "You know, they only get dusty again and anyway it's not just *your* hall and it isn't fair for you to have to do it. Honestly!"

The poor woman, looking at Doris's fresh face, blushed and apologized. "Now, it's nothing specially . . . once in a while only. . . . We're having company and yuh kinda like to have things perked up some, yuh know, when somebody's comin'!"

"Yes, you do, but still!" Doris would stand there for a moment in a neighborly fashion and then say, "It's awfully tiring, all this housework, and then it leaves so little time for anything else."

"Oh, I just let things go," the answer would be, increasing Doris's perturbation.

Parks's wife was an attractive girl, tall, athletic, wide-browed, with blonde hair as silky as pale satin, fine skin

34

and perfect, straight white teeth which had never needed a dentist's drill. Everything about Doris's face was of an almost magical cleanliness and clarity, a gift of nature which the hard-working housekeepers below, with their neat habits, could never have achieved. She liked handsome sports clothes, tweeds and checks, imported scarves, expensive walking shoes; she cooked the morning eggs wearing her best plaid skirt and pale cashmere sweater. But her dearest love, she would sometimes confess, was a well-tailored white silk blouse. "I almost hate to wear one though," she confided to her husband. "You send them to the laundry a couple of times and you've just about spent again what they cost originally. I wouldn't so much mind washing them myself, but the ironing of something like that is really frightful. Takes a professional to do it right." The blouses were a considerable expense and, furthermore, she had become here in Iowa a bit ashamed of sending so many things to the laundry. It was most embarrassing of all to have no answer when the washing machine was kindly offered. She did not want to appear in any sense different from the other women, but there seemed no way to establish perfect rapport without working herself to death. Her equalitarian heart, mourning the constant thump of the iron in the apartments below, did not like to have her neighbors view her extravagance, whereas she had no hesitation at all about letting them view her extraordinarily chaotic apartment and did not even notice their surprise. That Doris could no better afford the laundry than her neighbors was a secondary matter, which she acknowledged occasionally by a deep puzzled sigh and a few moments of concentration in which

35

she made up her mind to do something interesting which would also earn a bit of money. And so the blouses stayed in the laundry bag and occasionally when one of her trousseau suits demanded it she would buy a new one. "On sale, Joey. It's really a saving because white blouses never go out of style."

"It looks pretty on you, honey, just like that other one I've always liked."

"It is like it, but then they're all alike when you come right down to it. *Classics,* they're called."

"God, horrible name!"

"Yeah, I know."

On that interesting morning when he first heard of Rudy, Parks climbed the steps quickly. Quietly, almost stealthily, because he loved the privacy of the morning, he reheated the remains of last night's coffee, arranged his cigarettes and ash tray, made, as it were, preparations to read the amazing story in the newspaper. "Who on earth are these people!" he wondered again, disappointed that they had been beneath his nose for some time and he hadn't known them. Parks had a literary turn of mind and in fact he was, without the knowledge of his family, hoping to be a writer of stories and novels, rather than a teacher as his parents supposed. It was this dramatic, story-loving temperament which made him act so very peculiarly about the fascinations of the morning paper. He had merely glanced at the headlines and discovered their exceptional interest. His very eagerness made him tenderly fold the paper, put it aside until he should be ready with his coffee and cigarettes to give himself up to it entirely.

"How fantastic! That good-looking girl's dead!" He learned Rudy and Betty Jane had been to a dance at Rudy's fraternity and had returned to the rooming house later for a nightcap. Parks did not sympathize with the looks of Rudy, who appeared before him in last night's news photograph, a shot slightly out of focus, showing a pale, confused, and almost mindless face. No, this first glimpse of Rudy's countenance aroused anger in Parks, who saw a slinking, shifty-eyed criminal with his coat collar turned up, his hair blown by the wind, his features dissolved by the mediocrity of the photographer. And opposed to this trapped horror was that saddest of all things in the world, the death of a beautiful young girl.

"Joey," Doris said sleepily, but already laughing. She liked to affect a gruff, querulous tone with her husband, done in imitation of a nasal friend. "What are you doing over there? You know the smell of coffee wakes me up and I don't want to wake up at the crack of dawn, now or ever. . . . You're just like an old man. . . . They wake up that way and then sleep all afternoon. If I catch you taking a nap in the afternoon after this dawn business . . . Honestly, it looks like the paper would keep a while. There's never anything so pressing in it."

"A really amazing thing has happened, Doris," Parks said softly. "You'd never guess. Something absolutely unexpected. There's no point in even trying to guess."

"But I had no intention of trying."

"Awful!" Parks said, whistling.

"Who cares what's happened at this hour. . . . You

know, dear, you must get a hammer or something and try to mend this bed. It's a torture chamber fit for the Marquis de Sade! The springs or something are loose, sharp as a nail, and right at the top of the mattress. We'll be killed in our sleep. . . . These nails jut out and scratch you raw. . . . I read once of a woman who got up, half asleep, for a drink of water in the night and cut her foot without realizing it. She went happily back to bed and bled to death. . . . If we don't do something that's what is going to happen to us here. I'm afraid to speak to the landlady. She'll say we uncovered these spears on purpose."

Doris was fully awake now. "You're too fat, Joseph. If you'd get a move on and help me with the housework, you'd trim down a bit. We mustn't put butter on the potatoes for a while. . . . I understand potatoes aren't so bad by themselves."

Parks did not like these jokes about his weight. "Something amazing and terrible has happened," he said reproachfully, as if this justified his love for buttered potatoes. "It's really shocking! The last thing you expect in a place like this."

"What on earth? Well, let's have it." Doris propped herself up in bed, resting the pillow against the wall. She was wearing a pretty blue silk nightgown with a high bodice and short sleeves tightened by blue ribbons, an old-fashioned model which had, just a few months ago, come back in style. She was twenty-three and did not look more than sixteen—the smooth serenity of her skin, the health, the incomparable health in her blue eyes and gleaming teeth and straight, wide shoulders was lavish. Doris hadn't a distinguished face, it was rather too broad and innocent for that, nor a haunting face either, but one dazzling in its openness and utterly revealing of the plenitude she took for granted. No, she could not sew or cook or clean, but she could swim and dance wonderfully, loved walking and bicycling, and, after that, lying in bed, eating an orange, and reading with the aid of her black, horn-rimmed glasses. Sometimes there were faint lines of indecision on her fair forehead and occasionally a slight uneasiness in her voice. These would appear when, as she expressed it satirically, "things get a little too deep for me," by which she meant no compliment to the superior profundity of *things* but rather that she had detected a dishonesty or an affectation, two things she "detested." Doris had indeed, like her husband, a great many opinions which meant more to her than money, comfort, or even love.

Joseph looked severely at his wife. "It's dreadful, a tragedy, honey. A girl's been killed it seems or at least she's dead and has been since last night. . . . They were both students, the girl and the boy, and the boy's in jail. What do you make of that!"

"Is it true? You love crimes, all you sweet-natured people do. You can't wait for the papers just to get at them, deaths, political crimes, everything dreadful. . . . But I can't believe anything very striking has happened *here*. New York, maybe, but not here."

"Don't try to be clever. It's all in the morning paper and it is not a pretty tale, believe me."

"Is it something really awful?" Doris said, lowering her voice. She was not quite ready to get out of bed, but did so as soon as she realized her husband wasn't joking. Standing beside him, her hand on his shoulder, she looked at the headline and the photographs beneath it. "Oh, this is dreadful," she said, shaking her head. "I can't make out just what happened. Did they know each other well or just that evening?"

"You may be sure they knew each other well," Joseph replied gravely. "Very well."

"Students, too, poor things!" Doris looked very sad and thoughtful, standing there barefoot in her blue gown and robe. "Is there any more coffee, doggy?" she asked after a moment.

"No, let's make some fresh anyway. This last was pretty strong medicine, Madame!" Joseph said, pointing a finger at his wife, who paid not the slightest attention to his rebuke.

Doris made coffee and toast and it was just eight on the courthouse clock downtown when they had breakfasted, thoroughly read and reread the newspaper. This study sobered them, even though it could not be denied that the event itself gave a certain brisk and animated tone to the morning as any unusual happening will do. The day was now calm, bright, and cold. They sat by the window, quietly meditating, slowly puffing on a cigarette, immensely interested. Even though they were almost strangers in Iowa, they felt called upon to penetrate the girl's death and the boy's arrest in some special way, suitable to the accident of their being on the scene, that is in the same town. They expected and received many inquiries from their friends in the East.

Doris at last in a withdrawn, secretive manner said, "The girl's very pretty. Really *quite* pretty, don't you think?"

40

Her husband nodded solemnly. "And you know something else?" Doris went on tentatively.

"What else?"

"Well, she's not *just* pretty like almost every college girl, or at least like so many it wouldn't be any distinction. . . . No, she's more, this girl . . . she's sort of fashionable somehow, in a way a man might not know about." Doris was looking again at a snapshot in the newspaper: a sunny, winter glimpse of Betty Jane Henderson, standing in front of shrubbery that was heavy with snow. "A heartbreaking picture!" Doris said. Betty Jane was wearing a fur coat, no hat. She had a thin, delicate face and light hair combed back over her ears, on which she wore small earrings that appeared to be of pearl to the eye as sharp and serious as a jeweler's which Doris turned upon the photograph. She gave a mystifying amount of attention to each detail of Betty Jane Henderson's dress.

"Now!" she offered as a kind of scholarly conclusion. "It's not just the coat, not by any means, although from what I can tell it looks handsome enough. But still anybody can have a fur coat! You see, it's something else, something special in the way she dresses. Her skirt, which you can barely notice in this snapshot, her shoes, even the scarf, and her hair, the way she has it done . . . She's quite *smart,* in addition to being very, very pretty. They are not the same thing, those two—"

"What two?"

"Smartness and prettiness. She's almost like a model, but not one of the odd, horse-faced, elaborate sort," Doris continued industriously, seeking absolute precision. "Not the formidable type you know you can never possibly

41

imitate and who are chosen for that reason . . . This girl is the sort an advertiser would think of for simple cosmetics that don't cost a fortune, for shampoo, home permanents . . . that sort of thing. . . . She's got that extra little bit of dash and style, but still she looks like a lot of other pretty girls. Do you see what I mean?"

"I don't get quite as much out of this small picture as you seem to," Parks said fondly, but trying to suggest Doris's sociological effort leaned too heavily on clothes. He shifted to *his* line.

"There's every sort of sickening incongruity here," he said in his most thoughtful manner, leaning back dangerously in his rickety chair. "You get a terribly confused idea of this boy and girl, the fraternity dance, his rooming house, their relationship. Yes, that it should be one of those boring fraternities—that somehow makes it worse. You'd think State Universities could do without those things—"

"These schools are awfully big. Maybe these clubs and groups serve some purpose. Who knows? I'm not defending them—"

"Please don't—"

"Another thing, sweet—" Doris interrupted, still with some abstruseness and unmindful of Parks's desire to continue his own speculations.

"What now?"

"Well . . . Well, I believe, and I know a little about these things . . . I believe her sorority was a cut above his fraternity, if you follow what I mean. Better."

"No, I don't follow. *Better?*"

"The system's not my doing, pet, so don't be cross

42

with me about it. But still facts are facts and the fact is that there aren't *just* sororities and fraternities per se. Some are—there's no other word—considered better than others and I believe it's different in different places."

"You don't say!" Parks exclaimed. "More exclusive you mean? Take more money or more family or more clothes?"

"Yes, that's it and other things too. Don't make it too simple."

"I don't care to go into all this so deeply, to get the finer discriminations."

"And also—"

"A further contribution?"

"I firmly believe she was tired of him, but not exactly *through* with him. Girls feel that way. It's awfully hard to be through with someone who's crazy about you. They hint that in the news story—her uncertainty about her feelings. And I think it was really true. Hard to understand, perhaps, if you want to be pedantic about it, but rather easy with a little imagination."

"What's easy with imagination?"

"Being tired of him, but not through with him."

"Goose! How can you know? She's dead, that much is certain. It's shocking!"

"Yes, poor girl, poor girl," Doris said, her eyes clouding. "Really very *smart,* though I don't think so much in the way of brains perhaps. . . . And there he is!" She began to study an older photograph of Rudy provided by the newspaper on an inner page. It was more interesting than the unfortunate one taken at the scene. She saw his alert, pleasing face and fell into a revery about her own school days. It seemed she had seen this face a thousand times, gazing out of frames on the girls' dressing tables, face upon face, sweethearts and brothers, so like Rudy. "There's something wrong somewhere," she concluded wistfully.

"Betty Jane was an unsuspicious normal young girl of the happiest, kindest nature. Even as a little girl she was always warmhearted and trusting and got along well with everyone. She was not aristocratic in her outlook on life. On the contrary, she was very democratic, and accepted as her friends people in all sorts of different cultural and social groups. In a large State University you meet a great variety of human nature, just as you do out in the world. That's the risk we parents take, trying to teach our young people how to stand on their own feet. This is a tragedy of an innocent girl not knowing how to choose her companions. She trusted the wrong person."

This statement by Betty Jane Henderson's father, a prosperous banker in Des Moines, appeared in the afternoon paper. The disconsolate father was near collapse, the story reported, and had to be supported by his physician. And there was Betty Jane's house, a capacious, stucco residence, Spanish style, put up in the 1920's, and surrounded by a well-clipped hedge.

At the same time Rudy's biography was spun out for the public. It was as lowly and cozy as a fairy tale. The good, hard-working father at his lathe in a furniture factory, the family in a small, yellow frame bungalow with a geranium in the window and a spotless, shining kitchen where Finnish cookies were baked.

An extraordinary thing happened to Parks when he read

44

the evening press. He was taken immediately by a convulsive attack of party spirit. Mr. Henderson's statement injured Parks's dearest feelings and by some sort of whirling logic he became Rudy Peck's defender. Everything in Parks's being allied itself with the yellow cottage against the Spanish stucco, with the simple carpenter at his work against the Des Moines banker, with Rudy alive against Betty Jane dead. Because the desperate Mr. Henderson had seemed to hint that Rudy was not the social equal of his daughter, Parks felt that a great and ugly puzzle had been solved, or that the question had somehow been altogether changed. "Rudy was blameless!" he cried. Grand, helpless as a Greek hero, the young man accused of a crime had that primordial innocence of one mistreated by the gods, an innocence no transgression could deface.

After this first day when the girl's death became known, Rudy was in jail for two months while his trial was being prepared. "What a grim period," Doris said. "But I suppose he needs time, even alone in jail, to realize his new life. No matter what happens it will never be the same."

"I don't see why not! If it's all to be looked at as an accident he ought to be allowed to start over without prejudice."

"But have you noticed, Joey, that in a rape or an assault, even the victim is a bit looked down on afterwards!"

In the two months between what the lawyers called "the event" and the trial, Parks's fascination was kept alive by rumor, fact, and tireless speculation. And now at last the judgment and the answer were to be argued.

Snow gathered on the courthouse lawn. The sky darkened over the bleak town, miles of forlorn, elephant-gray front porches, doorways sealed against winter with oilcloth of a most icy, slick, black sheen. In the courthouse the window next to Parks was raised an inch or so and he felt the unfriendly wind upon his neck, just as before when the window was closed he had been attacked by the heat of the radiator. He followed the State's brief outline of the case.

Mr. Garr, the prosecutor, was a spare, durable, patient man in his fifties. The lightness of his voice, the serious, parsonish paleness of his manner—such were the materials of his personal drama, made from the negation, like a modest, faint-hued figure in a fresco who was nevertheless the main subject, as Mr. Garr was at the moment. This lawyer existed at the greatest possible distance from anything wild, windy, or even extravagantly intransigent, but still there was a certain reproach and condemnation in his presence, which arose not from verbal virtuosity of which he had no great amount, but from his whole effect, which was that of a good man. One could not imagine him with wayward or dull sons, or without sons either. Parks was truly interested in Mr. Garr but could not "like" him because of his role as prosecutor.

The lawyers on both sides had to deal with objects, the golden emblem and chain of a fraternity pin, with moments and youthful, familiar expressions of dismaying greenness, naturalness and typicality, the refractory language of college life—this *crime passionnel* played out in baby talk.

Mr. Garr continued. He believed Betty Jane Henderson had died from the wounds on her neck, which he meant to show were the result of the application of great, intentional force. The State believed Rudy had killed the girl, wanted to kill her too, because of jealousy and resentment that their "relationship" was at an end by Betty Jane's wish. The preceding summer her parents had returned Rudy's fraternity pin by mail; that same summer Rudy had made a trip to Michigan to visit Betty Jane and had discovered she no longer felt bound to him or seriously

47

interested, although they continued as friends. The increasing disinclination on Betty Jane's part was testified to by an act of expressive partiality: her sorority had entertained with an evening dance just the night before her death but she had not invited Rudy to this party. She had asked another young man.

"These dances again! Who can know what such ridiculous things mean!" Parks thought.

Near him he heard someone whisper. "These doings don't go well with the jury. They hate all these dancings and dressings up at the college."

Without even searching for a metaphor to strengthen his discourse, Mr. Garr paced on with his story, himself a deaconish ghost at the dances, partings, quarrels, the sore-footed postman with the rejected fraternity pin.

As Parks listened to this he seemed to hear another humble, portentous, disquieted voice, his mother's, repeating, "When I was your age I thought these trivial difficulties were a matter of life and death, but . . ." He sought out Rudy's searing, bright face, which was turned toward the prosecutor, whom he was following with ghastly attentiveness. "Is it possible?" Parks wondered, ". . . and if it is, how unfair, that he . . ." Parks felt ashamed for all the follies of his own youth and turned away from Rudy. Mr. Garr summed up shortly: with his exclusion from the dance, Rudy's jealousy and determination culminated fearfully and there at the end of it all was Betty Jane, dead.

The defense was in the hands of Mr. Brice, a large, rapid, brown-suited man who wore wide-brimmed, ample, beige hats and drove up to the courthouse in a vanilla-colored Studebaker. These tender, much cared-for pastel possessions perhaps indicated, deep in Mr. Brice's heart, a certain solicitude for the fragile and impractical, an affection for delicate, quickly soiled shades and things. Mr. Brice was much respected and admired, and so also was Mr. Garr. Both of these men had something of the nineteenth-century provincial power about them; they moved with ease, decency, and a consciousness of success and honorable reputation in a world they still treated as personal and decentralized; they knew everyone and were known to everyone. They had got considerable pleasure and profit from life and their voices commemorated Iowa, dear Iowa, for they were Iowans as a Frenchman is French. The townspeople could follow their contest with a local and private contentment with both sides, just as they followed their softball teams. Both men were thought to be intelligent and able and to this it was added with a smile that Mr. Brice, Rudy's lawyer, was "tricky," which did not suggest dishonesty, but a talent for flourishes of impulse. It was not unnatural that there should have been a great deal of hemming and hawing among the spectators, especially the older ones, some of whom were of extraordinary personal appearance, wrapped and bundled for the winter like Russian peasants. A few farmers of odd religious persuasion, the Amish, in their black suits, black hats, and neat beards, peered into the courtroom briefly, stealing a glance and leaving quickly, according to the dictates of their famous piety and industry.

Mr. Brice took the floor now and offered to the jury his impressive brownness, varied by a green tie. In a rapid, pleasant, untroubled voice he explained that Rudy and

49

Betty Jane were very much in love, "as the evidence will show." He turned and grinned at Rudy as he said this and was answered by a faint smile of unspeakable sincerity. Rudy's parents stared numbly at Mr. Brice's reassuring back, at this advocate who was now their most precious possession in life.

Mr. Brice saw no division, no unmanly petitioning on Rudy's part. He found instead a smooth romance, which he managed to suggest was nurtured by the vigorous objections of Betty Jane's family. These "young people" had intended to marry, but meanwhile resorted to subterfuge because some persons, including the chaperon at the sorority house, were in league with Betty Jane's reluctant parents and for that reason another boy had been asked to her dance, taking over what would have been Rudy's prerogative had Betty Jane considered only her own inclinations.

Rudy's fraternity pin climbed to glory in Mr. Brice's version: this was an object with wholly unique properties. It might mean, on a young lady's dress, no more than a corsage, or it might be as profoundly significant and isolating as a wedding ring. The little pin was clever, too, like the love letters hidden in a tree stump in old romances. In times of danger it might not be displayed openly at all, but would be gleaming all the more brightly on the girl's petticoat, hidden, still closer to her heart. Mr. Brice felt certain Betty Jane had regarded the pin as an engagement and that it had been returned against her wishes, and as he said this, one had the idea he, himself, had had some difficulty with Mrs. Brice's parents, and it was possible, from the involuntary blushes of the jurors, that even they could remember similar complications in the battle for their Mrs.

Rudy's defense had a fund of anecdotes gathered on the night of the girl's death, all of it like a rushing reel of vacation film: Rudy and Betty Jane now laughing, here talking seriously, there holding hands. Betty Jane on Rudy's lap in the taxi, or holding Rudy's overcoat, or asking for the time, or crying, "How wonderful!" when she first entered the rooming house that night at seven o'clock, before the dance, hours before their return at midnight and her death.

On that terrible night, what had Rudy done? He had asked her to call for him and go from his rooming house to dinner. When she arrived in her striped silk dress, fur coat, and the dust of sequins in her hair she found one of those "Happy Birthday!" scenes such as office workers sometimes have after hours, with the desks stacked with paper cartons from the delicatessen, and red ribbons around the typewriters. Rudy had arranged to have food sent over from a nearby restaurant and there in his room he had prepared a modest tableau—a flowered paper tablecloth, a bottle of wine cooling on the window sill, a white candle in the top of an empty Scotch bottle.

Mr. Brice claimed this effort was much appreciated by Betty Jane and there was no doubt it was welcomed by the reporters, these candlelight scenes furnishing their headlines in advance, providing handmade *fleurs du mal* for the Sunday supplements.

Mr. Brice was convinced Betty Jane's death was a tragic accident. She was such a calamitous loss that Rudy had become confused and made misleading statements. He had

51

not truly known what *had* happened in her last few moments alive and had voluntarily, before the trial opened, admitted himself to the local psychiatric hospital, where he was given drugs so that he might freely recall "repressed material" and talk about the evening. Mr. Brice delivered this last information briskly and finished off with a cough.

The trial began. Policemen came one after another to the witness stand, admitted their names, scratched their heads and computed their years of duty with the force, thoroughly accounted for themselves as in the beginning of a play a character is suddenly given a bit of dialogue which establishes his identity and fits him into the plot. Parks smiled dreamily, working out a little dramatic dialogue of his own imagining. ("Yes, I used to know him at Oxford, where I studied before going out to India for five years and finally being called back by the death of my father, which took place one month ago and left me in possession of considerable property, although there is, unfortunately, some tedious litigation about it going on at this very moment.")

Parks did not admire policemen, but he allowed that some of these before him were passable. However, he imagined all of them must be secretly delighted when a breach of order occurred which gave them opportunity for professional exercise. "What else is there," Parks asked himself, "except riding around in those cars all the time and sharpening your wits over a cup of coffee and a doughnut in an all-night diner?"

Parks's mind and opinions had developed slowly, which did not mean he was cautious, fickle, or given to intellectual unrest. On the contrary, moving slowly as he did, he felt an unusual amount of contentment and intellectual certainty once his character and visions took shape. Now, although he sometimes thought this could not be true of anyone, he imagined he hadn't been at all serious until he was about twenty-four; at that time he had the sensation of everything important and true coming to him all at once. Parks had a prodigious capacity for sympathy and this gift at last began to mold itself into opinion, whereas when he had been a young student he had sympathized *everywhere* and with *everyone* and therefore had been generally considered an intellectual "lightweight" by his friends. With his temperamental tardiness he was naturally never quite up-to-date and had begun to read Steinbeck just as the fashion shifted back to Henry James. In college Parks had thought he would become a doctor like his father and so he spent three unhappy years in this course, which he had to abandon because he couldn't endure the thought of the fourth year, and after that, after that. He graduated at last in history, but had a feeling of uselessness because he didn't want to be a teacher and he certainly wasn't a historian. Parks was not lazy—indeed he had, in addition to intelligence, a large endowment of muscular steadiness and sedentary patience—but still he couldn't find a use for himself and he realized the trouble was that he was all emotion, constantly feeling more than he could turn to account. He was aware of something uncomfortably unique about himself which, steadfast as he was, deflected him from every path. When he entered the Army he was in a state of shame and torment about his future, and in the Army he did no better, for he was impelled, beyond any reason he could express, to refuse to become an officer as he might easily have done. This was a radical action all of his emotion seemed to demand. He suffered in the Army from boredom and discomfort, but not from any resentment. Nevertheless, and even while not feeling *himself* personally slighted by life, he began to have an army view of society, to believe it unjustly divided into a cruel hierarchy. It seemed to him obvious that many people in America were deprived of opportunity, that there was a general abuse of power everywhere, a lamentable failure of democracy. He could even regret, so large was his heart, that he had not been born to suffer neglect himself.

Parks had such a sanguine soul that his melancholy notions did not make him surly or despairing. On the contrary, his new ideas were an unexpected inheritance which augmented his previous capital—sympathy, friendliness, and a genuine absence of brutal self-interest—and appeared to make everything he experienced significant. Still this was not a profession and he thought or hoped he might become a writer. At twenty-eight, with Doris as his bride, he returned to school to learn his craft, choosing Iowa because it was not in the East.

After the policemen, a few students from the rooming house came to the witness stand, saying yes they had seen Rudy that Friday night or no they hadn't. Parks's attention wandered. He observed with surprise that it did so and yet it wandered on, resting at last on the press table where a large group of reporters, with industrious indifference, wrote and wrote and wrote on yellow pads, or, in a lull, chewed their pencils or stared out of the window. The reporters aroused Parks's curiosity; propelled helplessly by this, although awkward and shy inside, he approached one of them at the morning recess. Not the grand, tall, black-eyed Chicago beauty, vivid and gleaming as the set of garnets that decorated her ears, twinkled on her chest, and clinked on her wrist, the star of the press table, who dimmed the red-eyed, sleepy men and even often outshone in magnitude the urgent, pleading light in which Rudy himself appeared—no, Parks did not dare approach her. But he did address a pale-faced newspaperman from a nearby town, a dim creature pinched and shrunken by the cold, limp, amiable, and not spoiled by the sudden importance which had, as he lay sleeping one night, been thrust upon him.

"Mmm . . . ," Parks said, catching his breath. "One of the old dads on the jury said he was against capital punishment, that it went contrary to his religion . . . which one was it?"

"Mmm . . . ," the reporter said, blushing and looking away, as if Parks's gaze were too much for him. "I think it's the old one in the boots, or who did have on boots when he came in this morning. . . . I think so. . . ."

"Quite interesting," Parks went on. "It shows something, at least. *They* don't even think they can kill the boy. . . . The State I mean. . . . Otherwise they wouldn't have let the old guy serve, would they?"

"No, they wouldn't at that," the reporter answered, gazing beyond Parks to a group of his colleagues who were standing together smoking. But Parks did not let him off. "I understand they dismissed a lot of good jurors on some technicality or other, both sides did, and that it's no telling now. And such an important, complicated case. . . . .

55

Well, it needs everything, the finest intelligence and grasp, you might say."

"It does that," the reporter agreed and drawing up his shoulders he slipped away.

Parks was left awkwardly alone in the crowd in the lobby. He felt compromised, standing there without a purpose, and had the idea he was being judged adversely. He would very much have liked everyone to know he viewed all this seriously, from a moral conviction, and was not driven to witness Rudy's desperation by idleness or a disposition to pry. With gratitude he noticed that an odd-looking woman in a red velvet beret, standing next to him and also alone, was searching her pocketbook for matches. Parks obliged and, holding the light, took in every feature of her long, thin, sharp face, her sharply arched eyebrows and large gray eyes. It was a peculiar face, pale and fixed, all of it strict and bony, a face of another century, not quite pleasing now, except perhaps to a connoisseur. Parks dimly felt called upon to accept the long, pointed face, as if it were already the object of unfriendly comment. And the woman too was long and thin and stiffly straight, of a rather melancholy symmetry. Except for her red beret she was in black—black suit and Persian lamb coat, thoroughly brushed and neat, of a somber, quiet effort at perfection.

"Very bad business," Parks said.

The woman hesitated before answering. "Yes, and it will be worse. You've seen them," she said, pointing to the jury room. "Very nice people, but it's not possible to expect them to have . . . the breadth, the understanding. . . ."

"You don't believe—" Parks said. "You don't believe he'll get a conviction of first degree!"

"Possibly," the woman said thoughtfully.

"You see," Parks said quickly, "the whole thing lines up so wretchedly. Here's this poor boy, her family looking down upon him, pestering her that he wasn't good enough . . . destroying the natural relationship, driving the boy and the girl to . . ." Parks did not know exactly *what* he wanted to say, now that he had the opportunity to speak.

"Yes?" the woman said, without much interest.

"You remember the statement the girl's father made which seemed to imply there was some social inferiority involved, or that if Rudy hadn't been the son of poor immigrants all this might not have happened. . . . It's so unfair and prejudiced it makes your blood run cold."

The woman's calm was undisturbed. She said, "I do remember some complication of that sort, but it's hardly at the center."

"Not at the center!" Parks exclaimed. He was annoyed, because his soul inclined to partisanship as his body tended irrevocably to a comfortable stoutness. He liked to get things clearly settled and when he had done so the threat of the slightest emendation scorched his nerves painfully. He explained Mr. Henderson's state of mind quite carefully to the lady in the black coat, recalling the bereaved father's very words without an error.

"There's the clue to the whole thing it seems to me. That's it in a nutshell, the family's attitude toward a perfectly presentable boy."

At just that moment Rudy was standing with his parents. Their lips were barely moving, as if they pretended to talk

57

while having nothing to say. A friend tapped Rudy on the shoulder. He turned about quickly and smiled gaily, in one of those gestures in which the body returns by instinct to the habits of happier times. In a second the blankness fell again and darkened the resolutely optimistic manner of Rudy's friend.

"I should think the poor creature needs . . . well, treatment! As we all do perhaps," Parks's new acquaintance said. "Psychoanalytic treatment."

Anita Mitchell, the woman in the red beret, remembered Parks several times that evening. His cordial image made her smile as she stood in the kitchen mixing salad dressing. There was every likelihood, she believed, that she would see him again as the trial went on, perhaps see quite a bit of him. Anita anticipated this possibility with pleasure and even with relief, because she did not like being entirely alone in the courthouse lobby, without a single acquaintance to bow to. This made her feel like some mad hermit, crawling out of his lair to witness an execution. It was terrible to her that such a notion should even cross her mind, since her feeling about the trial was of a tragic and pessimistic nature. She was compelled to think about the case, to attend the trial, as a sort of private investigation into the rushing, torrential waters of the unconscious, those treacherous lakes in which we are all struggling to swim.

This unlucky boy whom she did not know, Rudy Peck, had sunk helplessly into the boiling pools, pulled down by a great chain of instinct. There was no one to hear his cries, certainly not the jury, for these people represented in Anita Mitchell's opinion and indeed were asked to represent just that coarse grain of humanity in the average,

59

that tacit strengthening of society's repressiveness which was the meaning and use of the law itself. "Of course, I am not for a moment against the law," Anita would say to herself, frowning, "but still it is not a pure science and certainly jurors, these twelve people, are not a pair of scales. If we must have people decide these things, they ought to be trained for it, at least for a case of this sort." Anita believed Rudy Peck to be profoundly, grimly innocent.

Yes, she thought, remembering Parks again, it will be nice to have someone there I know. She had found Parks pleasant and polite, an agreeable sort of person to chat with, a stroke of luck. Anita nearly always felt a bit lonely and liked to make new friends. She made new friends, but somehow the statistical change in her friendships did not always register as a true spiritual gain and she would find that she was still thinking of herself as somewhat shy and lonely. But she could be rather gay about her condition, very charming about it, which did not detract from the reality of the complaint. It was not likely to abate very much because "loneliness" was the name she gave, not to the absence of friendly acquaintances, but to her unwillingness or perhaps incapacity to succeed in the relationships most easily available. Every profession or situation contains routine and "natural" social possibilities which are not accidental, as Anita imagined, but are as fixed a part of that life as the wages. And so the rich see the rich, the poor know the poor, doctors enjoy doctors, and drunkards other drunkards. Anita was married to George Mitchell, a professor of chemistry, but she found faculty life oppressive and since this *was* her life she was often oppressed by it and in rejecting it had to suffer quite a bit of self-reproach, anxiety, and displacement. Her evasion of faculty life was a subterranean thing, subtle and quiet as Anita herself. She was not bored or arrogant; she simply wasn't there. Her shyness was of a remarkable quality, pure and valuable as a gem. She knew how to live on the moon because she had, dug into the surface of her being, queer little furrows of worldliness, fertile trenches of high-flown perceptions, elegance, and desire.

Anita Mitchell looked somewhat older than her true age because of her melancholy air and stylish somberness. She was indeed only thirty and her husband, George, was forty-two. It was one of those reasonably happy marriages of opposites which appear to the outsider thoroughly queer and unsatisfactory because neither Anita nor George was able to present to the public that placid, intimate union of interests and habits which establishes the reputation of a happy marriage. Not that they quarreled, but they seemed so very "different." Actually in public they were alike, both a bit reserved, although not quite in the same way. Anita appeared distant and recalcitrant, self-sustaining and aloof in a manner which interested if it did not please. George smiled and expanded but with truly modest effect.

Mitchell was a calm, preoccupied man of decent, rather dim, appearance—neat gray suit, thinning hair, pale, intelligent eyes; clean, trimmed nails, comfortable shoes, pleasant manners without intrusion. He was perfectly forthright in speech, said what he had to say without hesitation, but he did not stimulate conversation nor inhibit others from having it without, after the first formality, including him. Everyone found him "extremely nice," exchanged greetings and soon went on without him, as if he were a prominent clock on Main Street which friends used for a brief meeting place before wandering off in pairs. Naturally, George got along well and was lively and happy with other chemists. But Anita for her part found that "nothing happens to me when I'm with these people." She couldn't sparkle or even, she imagined, be interestingly, confidently quiet; she merely felt lumpish. George's colleagues, or their wives at least, always said Anita was "very sweet," and certainly she was never impolite, having instead a stricken, pleading air that asked for forgiveness.

Anita had social gifts but they were, like her best china, not for general use. She suffered much from a passion for privacy, intimacy, confessions, and difficulties and in the little circle in which this was established, a pitifully small group, she was generous, helpful, and tireless. Otherwise she became stiff as stone when the faculty wives talked about rearing the children, lamented the grocery bill, or swapped a new recipe for creamed shrimp. And yet when she found one of her own—a personality she could not have described because she had confused her needs with the notion that she was fleeing from the "dullness and stuffiness" of academic life—when she met someone of her own sort she could have spent literally years pondering, with all the weight of her melancholy passion, his childhood, his financial problems and future. With these friends Anita was also exquisitely domestic and liked to cook dishes of foreign flavors, to shop all day in Chicago for a few precious tins of *pâté de foie gras,* English biscuits, and sometimes a little flask of Pernod, which she served in tiny portions because the Mitchells hadn't much money. What she couldn't endure was the weekly beefsteak, frozen peas, and bottles of blended whisky with her husband's colleagues on Saturday night.

When the Mitchells came to Iowa they were forced to rent a fairly large and thoroughly shabby ruin, a relic of the McKinley era, furnished with a dozen front-porch rockers, some old sooty, unhinged wardrobes, and a few iron-stiff, massive sofas done up in wine-colored plush. Anita shrank from the aggression of this scenery and never quite forgave the town for this first fearful image. Still the house turned out to be a blessing because both its size and expense demanded action. Anita got the idea of renting rooms to students and teachers and she succeeded excellently in this project. She chose her tenants with the passion and efficiency of a perfect bureaucrat selecting candidates for a desirable foreign post which required rare gifts of adaptability that could not even be clearly stated, much less learned. Only a person who had been there could know just who was suitable and that foreign country was Anita herself and her quiet but very real desire for a charming life. The boys who came to live in her house were pleased, as if they had had a stroke of accidental good fortune in choosing Anita; when the truth was that Anita had chosen them, carefully, patiently. She was quiet and seemingly indifferent and so they had no feeling of unwanted obligations. The boys sought her out, were always the first to suggest a talk at teatime or a glass of beer in the evening if they saw Anita or George in the living room. They liked her enormously and "didn't mind" George, who was always kind and hospitable and very often at work in his study. Anita cooked her dinners only for true occasions, a birthday, Thanksgiving. She did not manufacture "occasions" and so her entertainments never became a duty which bore down regularly with the harshness of a tyrant's benevolence.

Mrs. Mitchell was not coquettish. In her friendships it was not love she sought. She wanted charm, beauty, intelligence. What was hateful were the tawdry and shoddy and what she feared was that life would choke her with its overgrowth of these qualities—and not in other people only but in herself. Cheapness and mediocrity were the rule: she knew it. You conquered them in your house, your dress fairly easily if you had a little flair, but they sneaked into your soul without your even recognizing them. Vulgarity was what the tired heart aspired to in its passion for rest. Fastidious, elegant, a quiet little queen of a modest kingdom, it was nevertheless the soul Anita cared for most. She dreamed of a world ruled by a philosopher, not by an interior decorator, but still awaiting the millennium she served the gods by more than a little care for the amenities, by a tenderness for such "nice things" as she could afford. Not having been born to charm and conservative correctness, Anita had a convert's scrupulosity. It was her fate to know all about antique glass and to have very little of it, she would say with a smile.

Anita put such a fine point on things, going so far and no farther, that she was difficult for her husband to understand. She was a woman of fine intelligence and small ambition. This wormy combination, never in the spirit's best interests, gnawed at her nerves but did not invade her virtue. Her sensibilities were sharpened by these outrageous nerves, which were sometimes like little points of pain to be endured without a cry—this was the meaning of her calm, rigid manner. With the stubborn passion of shy natures, Anita clung to her convictions, whether it was Monteverdi, the "truth," or dead-white walls.

George Mitchell adored his wife, finally admiring her defects as precious eccentricities. His wife wasn't outgoing with his friends, didn't help his career, but Mitchell was a serious, hard-working teacher and felt no need for his wife's assistance. A generous man, he knew Anita did as she must. Only he had seen the mask harden on her face when they were dressing for some sort of University affair.

Anita's emotions were more deeply involved in Rudy Peck's trial than she realized. Here, right on her doorstep, was a ripe complication, imponderable, terrifying, and pitifully pressing. Since Rudy's indictment for murder, Anita had had difficulty sleeping and yet she didn't feel at all tired.

That night, the first day of the trial, she had a rather silent dinner with her husband. George Mitchell was one of the few people in town able to think of something besides Rudy, and Anita was often glad of this without knowing just why. It seemed to give her complete freedom, as if Rudy were *her worry* like the housekeeping, and a subject upon which she needn't suffer contradiction or interference or prohibition. Still she had had an unusual day and was urged to give out a bit of it. When they went into the living room for coffee, she handled her white, gold-trimmed cups with great caution because her hands were actually trembling. At last she took a deep breath and, flushing a little, said, "I have a confession to make."

"You don't say," George answered, pretending to be alarmed.

"I went to the trial today."

"You don't say!" her husband repeated. "All alone?"

"All alone."

"That *was* brave of you," George said, smiling. "Weren't you a little embarrassed? It's so hard to get you to go out like that . . . and there must have been quite a crowd and a push."

Anita shifted restlessly. "Yes, there was a crowd, but I sort of enjoyed managing it. At first I was shy and wanted to leave, but after a while I didn't mind at all. . . . I *had* to go and so I went. Now, it's nothing, really. I intend to go every day, I think."

"What do you mean you *had* to go? You're always exaggerating."

Anita attributed questions of this sort to George's scientific training. They irritated her sometimes and threw her off guard and she found she often said less than the truth, as now when she replied, "Of course, I didn't *have* to go, George, if you put it that way. It was only a manner of speaking and what I meant was that I wanted very much to see it all, I went to the courthouse, and now I'm glad."

"Why did you want to go?" There was not even a suggestion of criticism in George's voice. He asked questions for one reason only—he wanted to know the answer—and this, far from being simple, was one of his major eccen-

66

tricities with which Anita had to deal. Even she could never be quite certain that George wasn't probing for some deeper revelation, or that he shouldn't be.

"Why did I want to go, George?" she said, settling back on the hard sofa which she had covered with chintz. She sipped her coffee thoughtfully. "First of all, it's awfully interesting, you know. Really terribly interesting . . . and then its being right here, almost as if it were friends or neighbors. I've never been to a murder trial before . . . and then the boy and girl, students, people close to us and fascinating in their own right, not the usual run of criminals . . . and the boy, nothing like this has ever happened to him before. He's never been in scrapes . . . in fact, I hear he's unusually intelligent and serious. You see, dear, it's . . . well, as I said, it's something quite out of the ordinary."

George was satisfied. "Nobody would deny that! I'm darned glad you got up the spunk to go." Advising Anita to do this or that, always giving her friendly, undemanding encouragement was one of George's favorite themes. He was not sure just what he meant to encourage her to do, but still he was deeply moved by the shadow of the pathetic and the frightened in his wife, by the peculiar calm of their marriage, the quiet, orderly neatness of their childless life. George was not an introspective man and didn't come face to face with his regret that they had no children, but he had in a dim way come to see their marriage as something odd and his home as a special place, clean, silent, arousing condolence, like a hospital. "Yes, kitten," he said, gazing at Anita with his forthright tenderness. "Yes, you must go about town more."

Anita began to feel more on her own ground. Modest, she made no great claims for herself, but nevertheless there were a few subjects she had ideas about. She liked music and followed the best programs on the radio and even managed—being as competently thrifty as a squirrel—to buy a small collection of records. Her other interest was, roughly, "psychology" and she came upon this as naturally as she could carry a tune, for she couldn't remember when she hadn't had a number of bottled-up impressions about the dark, sad helplessness of people, and a recognition of purposeless actions and fears and their fascinating persistence.

"You know what I was saying about the boy and the girl, especially the boy who's on trial, and about their being normal, to use that *hopeless* word . . . or at least not criminal?"

"Yes?" In the evening light, George's contented, fatigued face appeared youthful and attractive. Anita warmed to him.

"It does make a difference, George, in the meaning of the cases, in the way you respond to them. Somehow it does."

"I hadn't thought of it that way," George said, taking off his glasses and rubbing his eyes.

"When I was in Europe I had an example of this difference."

Anita had been in Europe one summer with her aunt, seeing France, Italy, England, and Ireland, all in six weeks. It had been a depressing trip and she had hated every moment of it because the aunt, contrary to the usual dimensions of that figure, was neither rich nor pleasant.

The old lady had saved just enough money from forty years as a section manager in Marshall Field's to take herself and a companion, Anita, on a thrifty, dismal vacation. They traveled third class, stayed in dark, fetid pensions, met no one interesting, seldom had a decent meal, and spent most of the time discussing their very real money worries. Even the minimum accommodations turned out to be more than the aunt could afford. It was as if the old lady were not in Paris at all, but still at Marshall Field's, guarding the petty cash box, counting up the sales tickets at six, and everywhere accompanied by the ringing of store bells and time clocks. Still after all these years Anita had managed to reduce the aunt's grim participation and to think of the trip as an exhilarating experience and of herself in her best flowered silk and Milan straw gazing at Europe from a sidewalk café, with a dreamy, abstracted expression on her face from which the old lady, rattling currency beside her, did not detract.

"Aunt Mag and I were in Florence—the most beautiful place, George, I want you to see it—and we could make out just enough Italian to read in the papers that a woman, about thirty-five years old, had been murdered the night before near one of the famous old bridges. We were very provincial and the idea of a woman being killed in Florence frightened us, really haunted us. We thought of one of those stunning Florentine women, or perhaps a tourist walking along, looking at the river, and then suddenly assassinated. But in the coffee shop the next day we overheard some young Englishmen who had lived in Florence for a long time talking about the case. The murdered woman was a sick, horrible-looking, alcoholic prostitute, who had been in and out of jail, and went about with all sorts of bandits and underworld people and so it didn't seem so *unusual* that she had been murdered. It wasn't an unexpected circumstance or ending, you might say. It wasn't right, but still we relaxed when we found out who it was."

"Did they find out who did it and bring him to justice?" George said hazily.

"How should I know! I didn't follow it through to the end."

"Still, they should have, prostitute or not."

"Of course, George, of course!" Anita said shortly. "Nobody denies that for a moment. I was simply talking about the way the case appeared to an observer. . . . This death we've had here is so sad and upsetting because it doesn't seem to be inherent in the circumstances . . . and yet it was either an accident or it was rooted in the two people somehow, just where or how doesn't seem very clear, but I imagine there's an answer if we could get at the inner strains and stresses. . . . I was thinking today, they were both an only child, she the apple of her father's eye, I imagine, and he the joy of his mother—"

"Yes, children are that to their parents," George said. "Yes, yes, imagine that father's suffering!"

"That goes without saying," Anita exclaimed quickly. "But you see, the jealousy and fears, the inner wounds, the provocations. . . . This boy was driven—"

"I remember Betty Jane Henderson now!" George said suddenly. "I do indeed!"

"Oh, dear George, what *are* you saying now?"

"I'm saying I remember her, she was in one of my classes.

But I remember very little . . . a blonde, I think, and not called to distinguish herself in chemistry."

"I don't think I can forgive you for that," Anita said with a laugh.

"Forgive me for what, for God's sake?"

"For not remembering until now that she was in one of your classes, and then . . . Well, now that you have remembered you have nothing to tell me about her. . . . This indifference to the beautiful girl and to an amazing, scandalous death isn't the mark of a higher nature. It may be just what it looks like, indifference. Never a noble thing!"

"Look here, I'm sorry as hell the girl's dead. If I'd had a chance I'd certainly have tried to prevent the whole thing!"

"How funny you are, George!"

"Yes, they say people with no sense of humor are the funniest of all. I believe that's what you mean, as you've said before."

"I don't *really* mean it, George. What was this girl like besides not being a chemist?"

"There are so many of them . . . and you know they all look alike these days. . . . I guess it's that they're all so pretty. Aren't girls getting better-looking, all girls I mean? I don't remember this nearly universal beauty in my youth. . . . There were quite a few homely ones. Awfully nice girls some of them."

Anita smiled at her husband, even though his imperturbability sometimes tried her sorely. After a while, George went to his study. He was a prodigious worker, a mad one; he worked at his teaching, he worked at his reading with a solitary, weird, self-denying fascination. It was this exalted, extravagant devotion to the training of young chemists that Anita most admired in George. She was not interested in the content of his science, but she bowed humbly to George's love of it. His excessiveness, his spirit possessed by its theme, his character ludicrously concentrated in one point—his wife recognized here the greatness of this man.

Anita sat for some time alone in her living room trying to read. She was an odd-looking figure because she wore in the evening, made by her own hand, a longish skirt of tapestried silk and a little velvet jacket, a costume which was considered by some an affectation and by others a simple amazement, since she did her own cooking and dishwashing. Anita's love of these costumes, her demitasse in the living room after dinner, even her black hair which she wore unfashionably long and straight and parted in the middle did not pass without comment. People wondered where she got such "ideas," and were mildly annoyed by her attempts at "style." It was not such a mystery, however, for Anita had been in her youth rather poorer than most of the other Iowa faculty wives. She had lived a bleak Seattle life as the only child of seedy, dull, poor Methodist parents, who stayed to themselves and hadn't even the hearty conviviality of their kind. She was considered homely, which she had indeed been, a thin, dark, stooped, humiliated girl of immense diffidence, who had passed her youth with no comfort except reading and longing to get away from her family. Finally leaving home, with a business-school education, she went to Chicago and was fortunate enough to get an interesting position with a philanthropic foundation and through her office a great many unusual people passed who treated Anita with great care and friendliness. She saw that many of their wives were not "pretty" either, but had presence and originality and she set about modestly having some of her own and was a success, at least to the extent that she was not ignored. She might even have aimed a little higher than George, but when she met him and saw that he admired her thoroughly from the first and in the frankest, tender way, without ever indicating the slightest indecision, she married him gratefully.

A little after nine that evening there was a knock at Anita's living-room door. This door was always closed so that the lodgers might have a free, unobserved stairway. Anita recognized the knock. "I'm so glad it's you," she said, shaking the young teacher's cold hand. "Is it awful out?"

"Arctic!"

This was Harold March, who had a room on the second floor. He had been with the Mitchells for three years now and was a favorite with both of them. Short, spare, fresh, youthful-looking, with regular, somewhat petulant features, Harold March seemed to Anita as brilliantly undiscoverable as the bottom of the sea, a fascinating, multicolored, swift, rare fish.

"Are you busy?" he said. "Kick me out if you are. I thought perhaps you might have some coffee left."

"Yes, there's a little. Not very much though," Anita said, going for a cup.

73

Harold March did a lot of half-serious complaining and always with a bright, cheerful expression on his face. This good-natured grumbling made him quite popular because it meant he always had something to say. His air of sulky amusement was widely approved of. It floated about him like a dramatic theme, particularizing his general kindness and generosity.

"Do you think, tell me . . . do you think I'm mad?" March said, smiling.

"A bit, certainly."

"I'm really at the point of collapse now. I've quit smoking! That along with everything else! I love these battles of the will. It's the suffering that makes them so interesting. . . . But still that's not the real reason."

"What is the reason? Why do you stop if you enjoy smoking?"

"My reason is shameful. It would make everyone despise me if they knew. You see, I'm convinced smoking shortens your life, gives you cancer, and I can't endure the thought of that. But then I remind myself that everyone I like and admire smokes constantly and why should I want to outlive all the interesting people on earth. It's niggardly, but I do!"

"You'll take it up again. So don't worry about your greed."

"That's too much to think of. If I don't stick it out it will mean all the agony of these past two days has only earned me three or four seconds more of life at the age of seventy-five!"

Harold March liked women very much as friends but he could not achieve amorous feelings toward them. He did not consider himself lucky, but he could not imagine himself different. The amazing thing was how often people failed to recognize this fact of his life. He believed it to be almost embarrassingly obvious and yet even Anita did not truly seem to understand him. He felt like one of those puzzles in which the wrong answer may be reached by the most logical and convincing steps. And yet as Harold sometimes phrased it in his reveries he was "tainted with normality." He hated sloth and triviality and would have perished as a pioneer rather than live by his wits as a handsome beau in New York. "This is strangely to my credit," he would think, "since I am a Virginian."

Anita had ideas for Harold and thought him wasted in Iowa. They frequently had conversations which ran:

"You ought to go to New York," Anita would say.

"No, I've been there. It would be a catastrophe. In the little bars on 8th Street, or pulling myself up by my bootstraps and drinking on the East Side instead . . . That one good dark-blue suit, pressed threadbare, bow tie and crew cut. It's too much!"

"Or Europe, perhaps," Anita would insist, puzzled.

"God, no! You don't want to understand that I have to fight against absurdity all the time. If I spent some time in Europe I'd be spoiled in a month like an overripe peach. I know myself. The temptation to feel I'd accomplished something simply by being in Paris would be too much for me."

Harold picked up the evening paper, which was lying neatly folded on the coffee table. "Thy worries are greater than mine," he said, pointing to Rudy's picture. "Now, will you look at him! Hair combed, suit pressed, jaunty

75

smile. How horrible! But they'd surely give him the works if he came in with tufts of his own hair in his fist and the prison gravy on his tie! How silly it is for him to *have* to look as if he were going to apply for a commercial job. I wouldn't last a minute. . . . The very hint of an accusation and I'd look as wicked and bloodstained as Bluebeard!"

"But still," Anita said hesitantly, "if you're innocent, Harold, and have to go through this nightmare . . . If you feel innocent, perhaps you act so, and anyway you must make the proper impression. After all, everything depends on—"

"Innocent!" Harold said, smiling at Anita's stern and precise manner. "Is that possible? I'm not saying that he's *fully* guilty, whatever that may mean, but *innocence* is another matter. The poor dog, it gives me the creeps."

"That's just it, it does give any sympathetic person the creeps! That's the main thing, to think that this could be anyone. You or I might be in this same spot. That's what's so nerve-racking and he, alone, has to go through it all and God knows what may happen to him, without the most complete understanding, which hardly seems likely, he'll be doomed for life. . . ."

"But everything awful gives everyone the creeps! Several years ago I read about a mail carrier being killed when, of all things, a suicide leaped from a window and landed on this poor man who didn't want to commit suicide but just wanted to carry the morning mail. It's haunted me ever since; the thought of suicide is bad enough, but being killed when someone else is joyfully jumping out of a window . . . Think of it! *That* might happen to anyone, too. . . ."

"I didn't mean accidents of that sort; of course we all take thousands of risks every moment. . . . No, I meant what is so touching about this case is that all of us who have been mixed up about some youthful affair and have had the most violent feelings . . . There's hardly a person who hasn't *thought he couldn't go on* . . . and so on. . . . *That he would simply die,* and so on. . . . Or think of how we've all provoked people we loved to violence, or people who loved us. . . . And sometimes it goes too far . . . the wires get twisted, and something happens, quite out of character, not at all desired—"

"There's a wonderful saying of Nietzsche's which goes something like this: The consequences of our actions grab us by the throat, unmindful of the fact that we have meanwhile reformed."

"Yes, but should they? That's so harsh!"

"A while ago I thought you meant to say he was innocent and now you seem instead to be explaining how he might have been guilty."

"I do think he's innocent!" Anita said, trembling. "I do . . . and I don't, perhaps, in the most technical way, but in the real sense, the human one, the boy is harmless, a tragic, tragic person!"

"God, you are *in it, aren't* you!" Harold said, staring at Anita.

"I saw him today at the courthouse, at the trial. I'll never forget it."

"You were really there, pushing in with all the others?"

"It was all quiet enough—in fact, almost as if it were

77

nothing. It's so hard to tell, but I wonder. Do the people hate him? You see, what's so clear is that he's *perfectly* sane and normal, a good boy, more so than the average, one thinks. A sensitive face, but not what you would call *weakly sensitive,* either, not a person admirable enough, that you feel life was just too much for, that something terrible was bound to happen, no, not that . . . I can't explain what I mean. . . ."

"Yes, he's quite charming, quite attractive!" Harold March said, looking at the newspaper again.

"Attractive!" Anita said hurriedly. "Perhaps yes, but I'm not getting at anything so, well, unimportant as that. I haven't thought of that. . . . I suppose they really won't execute him, but I fear they'll put him in prison for life, or if not that, thirty years or so. . . . It's awful, you can't bear it, when you've seen him, seeming so much like everyone, just as he was before all this happened. . . . At least a few others must feel as I do. I see in the papers they subscribed money for his defense. . . . He, poor boy, couldn't do anything on his own. . . . I don't know quite how to describe it, but all of it, all of it . . . This love affair, so intense, his ego so deeply entrenched in it and so much wounded by the girl, or at least it may have been that way . . . The boy and his parents . . . There's some masculine vanity of a proud and natural sort that somehow, somewhere . . . It all goes back, back before the girl, I imagine. And I admire Rudy for going to the hospital, for putting himself in the hands of the psychiatrists before the trial. . . . That takes courage, doesn't it? . . . It seems that he didn't really know what happened that night and that he wanted to find out. I understand they gave him drugs and he talked freely, recalling, and if he hadn't felt innocent he wouldn't have risked that! How I would love to know just what he did say!"

"We'd all enjoy a confession, Anita! But that's just what the legal procedure is for, to keep us from ever knowing it all. You'll never have the answer, don't plan on it."

"What had she done that reminded him of the intolerable?" Anita said thoughtfully.

"Who?"

"The girl, Betty Jane, or whatever her name is—"

"You know very well what her name is! Perhaps she wavered in her affections, but still, Anita—"

"More than that. He must have been very insecure to care so much. That horrid little dinner . . . I can see it all. I'm sure there was a paper carton of cole slaw thrown in. . . . The wine and the candle . . . ."

"Are you in love with him?" Harold asked, in a half-joking way that made Anita uncomfortable. She suspected with real alarm that Harold enjoyed finding her mysterious and secretive.

"You care too much about being amusing," she said, scolding.

"Well, you *might* be half in love with him. These people out here are very appealing and when you add to their solid, unaffected ways something mysterious and baffling they are extraordinarily interesting. Even the girl must have had it. I don't say she was conscious that trouble was brewing, but that's just what's marvelous about her. Sitting up late at night with her girl friends, curling her hair in bobby pins, and talking about wanting to be

79

friendly with Rudy, saying, 'I like him, Janie, but I don't think I'm in love with him, really in love.' I understand she was very popular—"

"For that matter," Anita interrupted, "I'm sure he was popular too with girls or could have been if he hadn't been so deeply and maybe a little extravagantly attracted to this one girl. He certainly had many friends, he was likeable."

Harold sighed. "How do you account for his telling the student psychologist, quite some time before all this happened, that he had desires to do violence to the girl?"

"It doesn't mean a thing," Anita said quickly. "We all use the phrase, 'I feel like murdering,' don't we? Every day. And those feelings are common enough. We can't be called to account. He was depressed, jealous maybe, and might well have told the psychologist he felt like killing himself and killing her. But he didn't mean it!"

"And that first night, Anita, when he called the police and they found the girl dead. He was excited, had a little too much to drink, maybe, and he didn't realize the long haul before him, true. He said he didn't want to live any more and that he supposed that would be taken care of! He also mentioned, quite gratuitously, something about being the only person in the room, almost as if it all were a murder mystery he was reading. That's hardly the kind of excitement one has, say, after an automobile accident—"

"But this wasn't at all like an automobile accident. If you were in a room with a girl who died suddenly that way, from choking, you'd be frightened, no matter how innocent the circumstances. And if you were desperately in love with the girl, of course you'd talk about not want-

80

ing to live any longer, and if the police came in looking suspicious and you were young, a little drunk, you could sav anything."

"Perhaps," Harold said. He turned around and looked through the window behind the sofa. "It's snowing again. I almost broke my neck getting home. And the infernal wind . . . But still the snow's better than nothing. You know you're *here*, summer and winter."

Anita too looked through the gap in the curtains and saw the snow falling about the arc light. "He's in that prison now. It's only a little after ten, but I guess the lights have been off for hours. I don't know, maybe not. Perhaps he's at the window now, looking at the snow on the bare ground around the courthouse."

"Yes, sad. College life must look like paradise from his spot. And maybe it is, from any place."

"No, that part of life when you're young and free is *terrible*. I hated it."

Harold sat on for a few moments without speaking and then getting up wearily said he was going off to bed. "Are you sleepy?" he asked, looking at Anita oddly.

"No, no," she said immediately. "Not a bit. My only fear is that the house will get cold soon."

"What do you do when you stay up late like this?"

"I read or just think. The time passes so quickly."

"Ah, well, good night, Anita," Harold said.

On a Saturday afternoon a young man from another county, Thomas Drew, drove in his old but highly polished black car to pay a visit to his school friend, Rudy Peck. This trip to the jail had been pondered in silent anguish for some weeks; the visitor did not know whether it was suitable for him to attempt the meeting, whether such a thing was allowed, nor whether he could bear to see Rudy in such grim circumstances. He told himself over and over that he did not know what he would say, was not even certain he would be able to speak at all. And even when the decision was finally made, Thomas Drew did not mention it to anyone, not even to his young wife. He felt such pain about Rudy that he flushed and trembled when he tried to speak of him.

It was a bright day, needled with wind. The car slid past long stretches of icy, bare fields. Drew was an Iowa boy of twenty-five, with reddish, wavy hair and a reddish, earnest face, rather thin and skimpy somehow and noticeably intense, pleasant, and alert, a bit frantic too, like a squirrel. He had not had a very easy life, although he was more than usually content with it and lived this life with great seriousness. Drew was a young husband and his circumstances were of such typicality they might have come from a statistician's brain—he was deeply in debt for his new house, his new icebox, his new stove, his new washing machine. His apportioned dollars and cents went out every week with a regularity as sober and comforting as one of nature's rounds; he was also expecting soon his first child, completing without pause the classical purity of his being. Drew was employed by his father, who owned a garage and filling station. And someday the son meant to overwhelm his father, to cause the old eyes to glisten with joy; he would do this by getting the local Chevrolet concession. This was his dream. Drew and his wife had a five-room house of white frame, built by the aid of a government loan. This house, still smelling of new wood and fresh plaster, warm with newness like an egg, hadn't any shrubbery or trees to cool it yet. Indeed the only decoration in the scenery were the dozen or so other houses exactly like theirs which made a formation in the otherwise barren spot as birds sometimes do over the ocean. The Drews prized their house almost to idolatry; it was young and magical, turning up out of nowhere like their happiness. Daily, filled with wonder, they enjoyed their possessions: the dark-stained bedstead with matching bureau and dresser, their extraordinary kitchen range with its automatic oven regulator and its clock ticking away all day, their tables, dark and fluted, taking a high polish and giving back one's own reflection from their depths, the lamp with peach-colored butterflies on the shade, their little objects, a bright blue pottery elephant with a spray of cactus spouting on his back, a round basket of silver, a wedding present, in which hard candies were kept.

Thomas Drew had gone to school with Rudy for twelve

years until at last the war and college separated them, for Tom had not at the end of his service returned to school. Drew was not by any means Rudy's only close friend during those early years; still there was a special quality in their connection. It endured without strain, being comfortably founded on recognized inequality—Rudy was much more charming, popular, and imaginative than Tom, and yet Tom was charming, popular, vivacious enough to make a worthy companion. Anyway, Drew loved this childhood friend of his, now almost to desperation. Because of this love he dreaded seeing him, dreaded it with a speechless anger against fate. Rudy's arrest and trial—how could he think of it except as a kind of awful disfigurement, a wretched battle injury that made the heart sink? The concrete nature of Rudy's predicament, the terrible question, he could hardly allow himself to name. Sometimes he could not sleep and would lie awake silently smoking. His wife would touch his hand and say, "I know you must feel just terrible, Tommy. . . . Being so close and all . . . You feel just like it was your own brother, I imagine, and that is something terrible. . . ."

Drew was ashamed for not having gone to see Rudy before the trial, but it was the trial, Rudy's coming out of the darkness of waiting, that gave him the courage to try to speak to him. When he finally reached his decision, the trial had been going for several days and was now adjourned for the week end. The courthouse was closed for the afternoon, slumbering and quiet after the excitement of the days before. The whole place filled Drew with horror on this lonely, cold Saturday. On the brown frozen lawn in front of the steps a large white poster lay abandoned. Printed in bold red letters, the poster announced: COMPLETE COVERAGE OF RUDY! ALL THE FACTS AND DRAMA! DAILY IN THE CHICAGO MAIL!

The jail was in back of the courthouse, a square of red brick, not at all sinister, but instead rather modern and comfortable in appearance. The front section of this public building was used as the home of the jailer. This was indeed a bright and cozy spot, with clean, shining windows, starched white curtains, nipped in at the middle with a plastic invention adorned with red roses. Pots of ivy were visible on a table near the window and walking past the house a visitor might hear the sound of a radio, playing love songs, or see the jailer's wife, her hair in bobby pins, covered by a scarf.

Thomas Drew found his way to the entrance of the jail and, after a pause to learn if Rudy would consent to see him, he was taken to the cell corridor where, with his heart beating rapidly and his face ludicrously flushed, he reached blindly through the bars to shake Rudy's hand.

"It must be cold out," Rudy said, hardly looking at his visitor. And then blinking, suddenly recognizing his friend, his mouth froze into a painful grin, whether of joy or embarrassment Drew could not tell. "Tom! Gosh, it's good of you to come. . . . I'm so surprised! So damned glad . . . I can't tell you . . . It's been a hell of a long time!"

"Oh . . ." Drew said, swallowing hard.

Rudy stared at him, as if overcome by too rapid emotions, as if scolding himself for forgetting that this friend would, of course, remain faithful. For a moment, Drew had the idea Rudy was reprimanding himself for not having recently found the occasion to acknowledge Drew's existence. The friend wanted to tell him: that is the way it must be, and if it hadn't been for all this trouble I might have gone a long while without thinking of you either.

Immediately the scales rose and fell between the two as they always had and it was consoling that this should still be the case—Rudy far more gifted and promising; Tom, decent, industrious, his narrow, agile features already marked by the quickening pathos of the known, the local, the average which he honored without chagrin.

"Much, much earlier I wanted to come . . . believe me. . . . I was planning it all from the first, but it's so hard to get off. . . . Something or other always turns up. I wanted to see you. . . . Yes," Tom blurted out at last. "I was afraid I might not be able to get in here, but they were as nice as could be I guess. . . . It seems to me you look pretty well, pretty well." Drew's crackling, unsteady voice sounded his apprehension that he would either go speechless altogether or say something outrageously inappropriate. Goodhearted, utterly devoted, his nature was therefore familiar with a dread of misunderstandings. He was amazed to find Rudy looking so well and worried lest his sense of this betray him into too much levity.

"I've been here over two months," Rudy said. "A lifetime, believe me . . . But you do eat and sleep after a while, in spite of everything. The first days I thought I wouldn't ever again, but I was wrong. You keep going on, no matter what happens, I guess. There's nothing else to do. . . . The trial's a relief in a way. . . . It really is, Tom. . . . At least, I get out a bit."

86

"God, I'm sorry, Rudy," Tom said, shaking his head solemnly. "Damn it all, this is a hell of a thing to have happen to you. You know how I feel and all that. . . . ."

"Yes, yes, I know you're not through with me. That helps a lot. It sure does. . . . I knew you wouldn't run out."

A patch of sunlight trembled on the windowpane and danced on the bars. In the light Rudy's face appeared more puffy and pale than Drew had first thought. In his gray sweatshirt, woolen socks and loose slippers, he looked remarkably like what he was, a prisoner of two months.

"Lots of people have been to see me," Rudy continued after a bit. "I know I don't have to tell you how much that means. I just couldn't stand it otherwise. The fraternity guys have stood by me in a body, and then some others too. . . . Some people have collected money to help pay for the trial. . . . Some of the boys were here just before you came, but there's no one I'd rather see than you, Tom. . . . Not a soul in the world, honestly. . . . Good Lord, we go back a long time together!" Rudy hesitated, chewing his fingernail. "No, there's not a blessed soul I'd rather see!" he repeated, now smiling at his visitor. "I just can't find the words to explain it somehow." He grabbed Drew's hand again, suggesting his apology and regret for the separation of the last years. Even in the liberal, fluid landscape of Iowa, social tact, reassurance, the perfectly chosen note of humility were sometimes required to overcome the subtle difficulty between friends when one had been to college and the other not. In this way, college life, in spite of its conspicuous absence of elaboration, became comparable to the "great world" for the young who were

87

outside it. But the noncollege person mostly suffered from guilt and self-reproach, finding in his heart that it was ordinarily only his own lack of energy and ambition that lay between him and the college doors. Between Rudy and his friend there was this faint embarrassment. They feared to look too closely, lest they find their different experiences had damaged their old allegiance. Now there was also a mist of suffering between them that was not dispelled by Rudy's way of deferring to Tom.

Drew began again, searching for words. "I guess we've known each other for about eighteen years. I figured that out driving over here—"

"I hope that big mathematical problem didn't cause you to run off the highway," Rudy said, laughing.

"If it did I managed to get back on again in a hurry. . . . Yes, eighteen years. That's no little amount of time, huh?"

"No. I haven't known myself so much longer, come to think of it. But long enough!"

"And by the way," Drew broke in, blushing, "Mary sends her regards to you."

"Mary?"

"That's my wife. You two haven't met. . . . Isn't it hell how you get so wrapped up in what you're doing? I never even got around to writing you about being married or asking you to come over. I sure wish you and Mary knew each other. We talked a lot about trying to get together, but in the last year or so, after the war and all, it seems like everyone got so busy and you weren't back home much. . . ."

88

"Have you got a picture of her?" Rudy asked. "Mrs. Drew, I mean . . . Mrs. Thomas Drew . . ."

"Sure, I've got one. But it isn't very good. It doesn't even look so much like her, because it's just a little snapshot taken at quite a distance. I've been meaning to get a better one, a real portrait."

Tom took his wallet out of his pocket and thrust it through the bars of the cell. There was a wrinkled snapshot of Mary, in a summer dress and white sandals, a docile, pleasant-featured girl, brown-haired and plump.

"You did all right," Rudy said, smiling somewhat bleakly. "I must say I don't know what that pretty girl was thinking of!"

"Not bad for me, I always say," Tom said jauntily. "I swept her off her feet before she had time to come to her senses. She's a little on the heavy side at the moment, because . . . Well, I'm going to be a father in a couple of months, God willing."

"Congratulations!" Rudy said, touching his arm. "That's really wonderful news. First-rate! I don't imagine there'll be any living with you after it's born. You'll be strutting around so much you'll be too good for your old friends. . . . Let's hope it takes after Mary in looks!"

Tom laughed gratefully, relieved by Rudy's attempt to be as they'd always been, although he couldn't quite remember *how* they had been together. Tom yearned to be more clever, to bring forth at just the right moment a precious memory, an old joke, a gesture, but he could find nothing in his mind except their old street with the yellow wooden houses, women sweeping front porches, bicycles and skates on the lawns. He wondered if Rudy could hear the loud beating of his heart, knew the tears that were falling somewhere inside him. He felt limp from this wordless sensation of sunshine, scuffed knees, golden leaves, a squat, brown hound barking in the gray snow, leaping for rotten sticks. Ashamed, stupefied, he went on. "Are your parents all right?"

"No, they aren't well at all. But what can you expect?" Rudy said, his lips twitching slightly. "No, they're about dead, not eating, not sleeping. I tell them it will all work out someway, but they are just about to drop. To tell the truth, I almost wish they wouldn't come to the trial every day. It's so hard on them, but they are afraid not to, I think. It is supposed to make a good impression when your parents stand by you, but sometimes I worry so much when I see them it makes everything harder."

"Of course they want to be here with you. I'm not surprised at that. I'd come myself, but we just don't seem to be able to get away at the shop since we're doing all our own work without help now. Be sure to tell your mother and father hello for me, Rudy."

"I will, I will. I'm not likely to forget that, because they'll be so glad to hear from you, to know that you came around to see me. They were always very partial to you." Rudy coughed and took a cigarette out of his pocket.

"I see the great athlete's taken up smoking again," Tom said suddenly, feeling himself in safe waters now. "Remember the time of the bar bells and the mile run every morning? We were at it all the time. Sending away for those chest expanders—"

"And both of us pretty lousy too, especially in baseball I remember."

90

"Speak for yourself!" Drew said gaily, abominably threatened with an explosion of giggles.

The deputy sheriff came in and spoke briefly to Rudy, who turned to explain to his friend. "There's a reporter outside who wants to come in—"

"Do you talk to them?"

"Yes, I nearly always do when they ask. It looks bad when you don't . . . and when you do, whatever you say looks awful in the newspapers. There's no end to the worries—" Rudy said nervously.

"Oh, God, Rudy, I'm right there behind you, you know. If there's anything I can do ever—"

"Thanks, thanks. I guess they don't mean to hang me. There are some folks on the jury don't believe in that, but I'll sure be glad when the trial's over. At least I think I will. . . . This waiting around for it to begin was terrible."

"You've got good lawyers, I hear, some of the best in the state, people say. I guess these guys are pretty smart and can be of a lot of help in these things."

"Yeah, the lawyers are swell, I'll say that. In that respect, call myself very lucky, very lucky," Rudy said, his melancholy lifting a bit.

Tom touched Rudy's sleeve. "I'll be going along. Ah, don't worry, boy. All the best, you know."

"Thanks," Rudy answered. "I wonder which one of the reporters this is. It's hard to keep them straight. There's even one from Canada! That's pretty embarrassing, this woman coming from so far away."

"Well, so long again," Tom said, turning away.

"What will any of it be like?" Rudy said in a low voice.

"I mean what will they decide. You don't know what to expect."

"It'll work out. It must," Tom said, moving away now, passing the reporter who was waiting at the end of the corridor. The reporter was rubbing his cold hands together and looking impatiently at his watch.

"Oh, Tom!" Rudy said, calling out to the last view of his friend.

Mr. Garr, the prosecutor, pressed his spectacles firmly on the bridge of his nose and went about the day's business. Just now he had Dr. Lawrence on the witness stand. Dr. Lawrence was a local physician often called upon by the police.

Mr. Garr had a large bundle in his arms. "Were these articles of clothing worn by Miss Betty Jane Henderson the night you were called to the rooming house on Carson Street?" Mr. Garr asked, with a sad, meditative expression. This attorney, mild-mannered and light-voiced, appeared to have the habit of deliberation in his very bones. His ponderings were not dramatic nor especially eloquent and still they seemed to impress everyone with their seriousness. Even in the crowded courtroom Mr. Garr could sometimes give the impression of being alone and quietly gazing over a stretch of land, thinking his thoughts, as the farmers said.

"Yes," Dr. Lawrence replied. Mr. Garr, with a puritanical distaste for drama, cautiously placed the mortifying bundle on the table near the jury. It contained Betty Jane's striped evening dress, white gloves, silk stockings, gold slippers—all wrapped in a sheet. Rudy was sitting with his lawyers at the same table. He blushed purple and lowered his head.

"Do these color photographs taken by Detective Smith give an accurate representation of the condition of the girl's throat when you saw it?" Mr. Garr went on.

Dr. Lawrence examined the photographs and said, "Yes, they give an accurate representation of what I observed." These also were placed on the table for later distribution to the jury, in spite of Mr. Brice's objections that they were "inflammatory, exaggerated, and prejudicial."

Dr. Lawrence, a regular-featured, middle-aged Iowan, set apart only by a pair of dark, pointed eyebrows that shot up like a decoration over the smooth portico of his silver-framed glasses, offered his recollections. He had been called by the police, he said, and found the girl already dead when he arrived at the rooming house. After that, he accompanied the police and Rudy to the station.

Mr. Garr nodded and shifted to another consideration. "At the station, Dr. Lawrence, did you attempt to take a blood specimen from the defendant, Rudolph Peck?"

"Yes, I did."

"What did the defendant say at that time?"

Dr. Lawrence in a rather toneless voice said, "Well, he kind of resisted the idea of the whole thing. Didn't like it."

"What did the defendant say when you wanted to take the blood specimen?"

"He said, 'I know what this is. It's truth serum. You're trying to trick me.' However, I assured him it was only a routine matter and then he agreed and gave the specimen."

"At that time, did Mr. Peck mention anything about a confession."

"Yes, he did."

"Will you tell the jury what he said, please?"

Dr. Lawrence turned to the jury and said quietly, "This young man said, 'Give me a confession and I'll sign it. I must have done it. Who else could have?' "

"Did he actually sign this confession, Dr. Lawrence?"

"Not just then. Later a statement about the events of the evening was drawn up and presented to him by the police. He signed that, but only after insisting that it be altered to say he was not certain about all the events of the evening."

"Did he mention *playing a game?*"

"Yes. At one time or another he said he and the girl had only been playing a game. In this game you try in fun to show how a person might be choked, or at least that is the idea I got of it."

Rudy's lawyer, Mr. Brice, took over here. He was in a thoughtful mood this morning, his whole manner faintly mischievous, hinting at original and interesting notions discovered during the week-end recess. Yes, Mr. Brice looked very spruce and confident this morning, one admiring lady observed in such a loud voice that the judge scowled. There was a high shine on the lawyer's shoes and his hair was newly trimmed. Dr. Lawrence could not conceal the quick smile that escaped from him when Mr. Brice approached. The physician was not Rudy's witness—Mr. Brice's manner acknowledged as much and having done so made his jovial grin for Dr. Lawrence appear as a gift he was offering an enemy.

95

"Well, sir. Now would you say this boy here," pointing at Rudy, "was he excited and confused when you saw him that evening?"

Dr. Lawrence hesitated. "Uh . . . Well, yes, he was certainly excited. Yes, I think you could say that much definitely."

"Yes, yes," Mr. Brice agreed hastily. "Did he show concern and grief for Betty Jane Henderson during this time when you had an opportunity to observe him?"

Again Dr. Lawrence hesitated. "I find it difficult to define such states of emotion with precision. . . . Yes, he seemed worried and upset, most definitely. Whether this showed concern and grief for Betty Jane Henderson, as you expressed it, I wouldn't want to say."

Mr. Brice came a little closer to the witness box, almost as if he imagined Dr. Lawrence's hesitation came from some difficulty in hearing the question. But when he spoke again, Rudy's lawyer surprised everyone by shifting his ground entirely. "Dr. Lawrence, did you have occasion to say in conversation with some of your friends or acquaintances that Miss Henderson's life might have been saved if a doctor had arrived more quickly?"

Dr. Lawrence looked astonished. "No, I did not!"

Mr. Brice stroked his chin. "Well, then, perhaps I ought to put it a little differently. In your professional opinion, could the life of this girl have been saved if she had had prompt and proper medical attention?"

"That's very difficult to say."

"What would be your opinion?"

"Of course, a doctor never knows about those things. It is possible, *possible* only, mind you, that if a delicate

96

and difficult operation had been performed immediately, an operation that would have allowed the girl to breathe, she might have. . . . I mean then her life might have been saved. It's only a theoretical possibility and I don't even know that could be said definitely for this case, even as a possibility."

"How quickly would such an operation need to be performed?" Mr. Brice wanted to know.

"I don't know. Very soon after the breathing was cut off. I don't know exactly. It's just a technical possibility. . . ."

Dr. Lawrence looked distinctly uncomfortable, fearing some trick was being played on him.

Mr. Brice rushed on. "Now, Dr. Lawrence, please. How long was it after you received the call before you got to Carson Street? I mean how long before you were actually on the scene?"

"I suppose it was twenty-five minutes, thirty maybe. You mean from the time I got the call? That's only an estimate. It may have been a little shorter time or a little longer."

"About thirty minutes!" Mr. Brice said in a clear, triumphant voice as he walked away from the stand.

Dr. Lawrence was dismissed.

Mr. Garr tacked a medical drawing of the human neck on the wall behind the witness box and called the pathologist, Dr. Rako, who had performed the autopsy on Betty Jane.

Dr. Rako had an olive-pale face and large, brown eyes —a sturdy, stocky man with some sweetness, even softness about him. His unhurried, wistful indoor softness was of the sort one often finds in a good shoemaker. With the medical drawing and Mr. Garr's careful questions, Dr. Rako explained the nature of the injuries, announcing the whole matter in his own language and with such confident simplicity that the audience could imagine for the moment it understood what he was saying. He said the autopsy revealed fractures of the hyoid bone and cricoid cartilage. The top of the larynx had been closed off by extreme swelling.

Dr. Rako was a pathologist and his information on this subject was to be expected. But there were many crooked smiles of pride and a few of sheer comedy at the dazzling authority with which the lawyers went at the anatomical evidence. They might have been anatomists themselves, as they tossed that science into the realm of speculation, made its laws appear purely personal, as uncertain as a witness trying to establish the time of a telephone call.

"In your opinion, Dr. Rako, what was the cause of the death?" Mr. Garr demanded. Sighing, he turned his sober countenance toward the jury and the spectators, reminding them that this was the real question at last.

The court waited. Dr. Rako said, "Asphyxia, I would say was the cause of the death. Asphyxia is a condition which occurs when the body is deprived of its normal supply of air. That seemed to be the situation, as I found it."

Mr. Garr looked disappointed and spoke more impatiently now to the soft and mellow pathologist, Dr. Rako. "Well, doctor, tell us what in your opinion caused the asphyxia."

There was a sort of whistle in Dr. Rako's voice as he

98

began upon this question. His great brown eyes seemed to wink bashfully at the jurors, apologizing for the uncommon nature of the studies to which he was attracted, the mysteriousness of his calling. "What caused the asphyxia, you say? It was caused by the obstruction of the airway in the region of the larynx and, more specifically, in the region of the glottis."

Mr. Garr peeked over the rims of his glasses. "What caused the obstruction, would you say?"

"Swelling."

"What produced the swelling that blocked the air passage?"

Again the listeners looked up in anticipation. Dr. Rako shrugged his shoulders. "The probable reason was that force had been applied to the neck area."

"Thank you, Dr. Rako," Mr. Garr said in an emphatic voice.

Mr. Brice, on Rudy's behalf, had his own anatomical dialogue with Dr. Rako. This exchange covered the same ground and Dr. Rako's bland prosiness remained undisturbed. Still somehow Mr. Brice seemed to end up with the admission that a simple sneeze had been known in medical history to cause similar fractures.

Parks was watching this morning from a seat in the front rows, a piece of good fortune which quite overwhelmed him. In his lucky vantage point, his face beamed above the crowd naturally and recklessly as a target. His rapid expressions, his frowns and smiles, revealed at every turn his powerful opinion about the witness on the stand, the

99

nature of the questions, and the course of the trial. But even when Parks was disheartened, his image was a warm one, a beacon announcing a friendly heart and all the time in the world to devote to other people's problems. He was the person nearly always chosen by a stranger in need of directions—and rightly, for he was as obliging as he appeared. Inwardly, Parks was feeling a bit nervous at the moment and wondering why this should be so. It was a mystery to him the way his spiritual metabolism tended to run amuck.

Parks had been put to quite a bit of trouble to get to the trial this morning. Early riser that he was, he still did not like to be on his way so promptly. Indeed any great movement at all was quite contrary to his purpose in getting up before others—he wanted those early moments for musing, not for dashing about. Today he had found it necessary to arrive at the courthouse before seven because each morning more and more people had the same desire he had to spend some time in the exciting comfort and warmth of the courtroom. And because of his studies he would have to forego the afternoon session entirely. Parks was very much depressed by the medical testimony; he thought he would have preferred not to hear this part of the case because there was nothing he could feel about it. He could only shudder and be relieved when the testimony moved on to other matters.

During the recital of bruised throats, broken bones, closed larynxes, Parks began quite suddenly to criticize himself. What am I doing to help Rudy Peck? he asked himself boldly. A man, a sincere one, ought to exert himself immediately against suffering and injustice, ought somehow personally to stand against it, make a sacrifice, prod the lazy spirit, fire the cold heart. It was terrible the way one's interest flagged, the way resolution diminished in that moment between the inclination and the effort. It was this that kept the world on its tired, cruel track, this endless and huge dissipation of the instinct for goodness and sacrifice, the way it simply spent itself without result day in and day out, century after century, died in heart after heart between breakfast and dinner. Slowness and indolence on behalf of justice, this he felt was mankind's great crime rather than a love or need for sheer evil. But how tricky and cunning it all was: the devil was surely just that incapacity for thinking of the proper sacrifice, the useful, courageous action. Only the puniest deeds occurred to Parks in this instance of Rudy Peck—perhaps he should send him a book, always if necessary keep remembering to send him books or cigarettes, showing an incorruptible fidelity, never quite divorcing himself from this wounded life. But what paltry heroics, what grotesque sacrifices, what a pitiful Abraham they showed him to be, and he would not even remain true to those pinchbeck offerings! Better than all, he wanted to save Rudy, to free him. The wish, at least, was pure.

When the time came for the luncheon recess, Parks loitered about in the halls of the courthouse, moody, smoking a cigarette, wondering if perhaps he might cut his school classes again in the afternoon. That he had been over this temptation several times in the morning and decided against it, even decided against it a further time just now, irritated him. He would tell himself, without conviction, that this "experience" was far more useful to him than anything he might learn from a lecture that afternoon. As he stood there, Rudy's parents passed before him; stooped and silent, breathing heavily, they came so near to Parks the smoke from his cigarette touched their humbled heads for a moment.

Parks was almost paralyzed with emotion when he saw Mrs. Peck's hand, long fingers, white and blotched with red, as if the hand were in pain. And the father—Parks's eyes met his. Mr. Peck's left eye was streaked with red, a sore, exhausted eye. Their very skin is bleeding! Parks thought with horror, as if these two miserable people were living in some dreadful, incredible, medieval tale. Giddy with identification, he wished he might be in Rudy's place, or almost wished it. It seemed to him that Rudy had nothing and he, Parks, everything. Somehow, somewhere these awesome deprivations, these souls born under a painful, scorching star—all this had to change or the world would go mad.

Mr. Peck, the old man, had been a factory worker all his life and this was the end of his uncountable hours of labor, this his soaring finale. A modest life at last horribly brought to public notice, its nothingness shattered forever. Crushing out his cigarette, Parks hurried down the steps after Rudy's parents. Catching up with them, he said in a vanishing voice, "I'm so sorry. I had to speak to you. Good luck!"

Mrs. Peck whispered, "Thank you." Her tired, anxious face was still for a moment as she gazed at Parks without cordiality, without gratitude, giving him only this stillness and the blueness of her eyes. And then, almost coldly, she turned away. The parents walked on, the mother faster, always ahead, and the father trailing. Parks felt rebuffed, but it was hardly a second before he asked himself what he had expected. He could only answer that he found much to admire in this unsmiling, withdrawn woman. Her attitude was so clearly "proper" that Parks's feeling of disappointment vanished.

Parks buttoned his gabardine coat and went out into the cold air, walking down the courthouse steps with rather a slower step than usual, a sort of ennui seizing him. At the moment he felt envious of all the tired, thoughtless people in the world, envious of the tired arches of clerks, the aching sleepiness of truck drivers, the freezing nose of the traffic cop. These afflictions seemed light beside the weight of emotion Parks was doomed to carry about with him. He never admitted, of course, the extraordinary intensity of his feelings. It contented him to be recognized as a "liberal"—he did not care for anyone to share the depths with him.

Alone now, with that despair and ennui biting him, he thought of Doris. Her ways were a comfort to him, being enough like his own to give him a feeling of solidarity and ease. And yet Doris was different enough to arouse the necessary admiration in Parks's soul, even to cause him to wonder how such a person as Doris could truly be. He hardly hoped to emulate her more astonishing qualities— that sturdiness which falsely appeared to be his too. Doris would certainly have spoken to Rudy's parents, and possibly to Rudy himself. Without the slightest constraint, she would have turned her alert, shining, unabashed face toward them, as if she were a brisk, sympathetic nurse at the bedside. Warm, natural, bold, no unsteadiness pushed up from the bottom of Doris's being—at least Parks had never seen it. But he! Right now he was trembling with a strange fatigue of soul which the short exchange with Rudy's parents had brought down upon him. It was humiliating, but fortunately no one need know it besides himself.

On the street below the courthouse, Parks saw Anita Mitchell walking toward him. Her long-featured, exclusive face was more bleak and harried than he had remembered it, but this new vision only made Anita seem more uncommon. Yes, she remembered him, she said, awkwardly stopping to greet him, the wind tearing her eyes. In the sunlight Parks noticed dark circles beneath Anita's eyes, twin arcs of delicate purple.

"I wasn't sure—" Parks said, staring stupidly, unable to find anything to say, shifting from one foot to the other, his arm now brushing against Anita's as he put his hands in his pockets.

"Nobody ever forgets other people. At least not so soon," Anita said. She smiled, one of those meager, queer smiles that touched Parks's heart. A mutual sorrow and fear seemed to pass between them most strangely there on the gray street. In the freezing, sun-specked wind, their faces turned white.

Neither of them saw that Rudy, accompanied by the deputy sheriff, had come softly down the steps behind them. He was making his way back to the jail for food and rest before the afternoon resumption of the trial. Neither he nor the sheriff wore an overcoat. In the cold wind both of them shivered and quickened their steps.

"Have you had lunch?" Parks asked shyly, watching

Anita's cold, intense face. She said she had not and he led her around several corners, through a brown and green metallic façade that shone clear and tinny like a great touring bus, into the restaurant, a diner affair where girls in hairnets and apple-green smocks served up hot plates of mashed potatoes and fried steak.

"What luck it is to find an empty booth," Parks said. "These places usually fill up around noon."

"Have you been here often?" Anita said, showing genuine curiosity about the answer.

"Just a few times, and those only because it was near the courthouse." Parks knew Anita thought this a dreary choice and he felt a little ashamed. The answer he gave was literally but not metaphysically true. The small number of times he had been to the diner did not at all indicate his feelings about the place, which were cordial.

Anita had not attended the trial in the morning because all the seats were taken by the time she arrived: such was the vigor, devotion, and promptness necessary to follow Rudy's destiny at firsthand. Being disappointed, she had not returned home, however, but had wandered to the library, and now was back at the courthouse hoping to make the afternoon session. With a deprecating shrug she expressed herself almost insulted that she should be deprived when the stupidly curious had their own way. "I suppose it's ill-natured of me, but I got a good look at some of the people and I couldn't divine any deep, serious interest in the case. Many of them are just the sort you'd see hanging around the courthouse any time. Of course, I'm annoyed and so I don't judge my rivals charitably."

The restaurant was uncomfortably hot and crowded,

groaning under the weight of radio noise and the clatter of dishes. Parks, looking around, saw that the clients today were rather a depressed looking bunch of citizens, humped and taciturn, colorless as the gravy.

"They like to rush you in and out in such places, but I won't let them," Anita said, studying the mimeographed menu and maliciously ignoring the impatient, buck-toothed waitress who waited, mouth open, teeth expectant, for the orders.

Parks enjoyed this place and was not offended by the unmitigated shine of the decoration, the harsh, tough shine of aluminum. He was attracted to it because it *was* metallic, hot, crowded, and popular. For his own taste there was too thick a coating of meal and grease on the cutlets, but still he imagined it was just this caloric liberality that made so many working people stop here, so many dusty truck drivers with caps pushed back on their heads. He did not even always mind the noise, although he rued its origin in the radio, that fraudulent, threatening Meistersinger, king of commerce, seducing an unhappy world to a frenzy of desire. In such places Parks proposed to study the Middle West, to lay bare the beating heart of Iowa. But what a uniformity there was in America, those Main Streets alike from Cape Cod to Texas, the national short-order cuisine spreading from coast to coast, inclusive as the Constitution—poor Parks sometimes did not know just what he was discovering.

"There won't be anything unexpected in the fare here," he said lightly to his companion. With heroic dignity and persistence, Anita was questioning the waitress about the various dishes listed on the menu, the brand of the mayonnaise.

Parks felt some disquietude in Anita's presence and yet he had no desire to run away, nor even to shorten the meeting. He very much wanted Anita to like him.

At last a chicken sandwich and coffee were ordered. Parks was tempted to break the ice, to rush at Anita with his prodigal advice and solicitude, perhaps to take her hand and say, "That's why you're so thin and mournful. You don't eat enough." However, he restrained these attentions, finding that his own appetite was skimpy today.

Anita arranged her hands on the table. "This wretched weather," she said. "I'd like to get away from it for a bit, but one of the most remarkable things about Iowa is that it's so far from wherever one might wish to go. It's only near other places just like it."

Parks considered what he might reply to this. Meanwhile, Anita continued, "What happened this morning? You were there, you saw it."

"It was mostly taken up with medical testimony."

"What did they say? How did it strike you?"

"It was dismal," Parks said with feeling. "The usual thing. They brought the girl's clothes—"

"Ah, me, not really!" Anita said, horrified.

"Yes, I'm afraid yes. The things she was wearing that night. Some effort was made to justify this, having the clothes identified, you know. And then photographs of the girl, after she died, of her throat, maybe even some secret pictures . . . these were passed out to the jury. It's not hard to imagine what sort of effect all this will have. It's all puzzling. Trial procedure is probably fairly cut and dried by now . . . based on the wisdom of the centuries they like to say, but it's far from perfect. . . . I have no doubt some sort of mean of justice is reached in the long run, if you took an average of the cases. A particular case may suffer under the best system. . . . Even the question and answer method is not a simple matter, not necessarily ideal in every instance. Sometimes it prevents the most important testimony from being heard and brings out the trivial instead. . . ."

"There's nothing to be done about that," Anita said curtly. "One would need a great deal of experience to judge such a matter. . . . Who did the testifying this morning? Every day people hint that Peck himself may be called suddenly, but I don't take it seriously at this point. Most of the reporters seem to think he won't be on the stand until the end."

"No, he certainly wasn't called this morning. Today they had the doctors, largely the man who did the autopsy. He talked about the bones, the windpipe, all the structural nature of the injuries. Naturally, I don't believe the jury understood very much of this performance. . . . It is technical, all this information, and you come away from it with impressions, but who is to say they are the right ones? I will say that the doctor who did the autopsy was extremely fair-minded. The prosecutor kept trying to get him to say the girl died because she was choked by human hands . . . Peck's of course. . . . But the doctor didn't quite say that, not exactly. He stuck to the scientific facts admirably."

"What did he say?"

"He finally said . . . and it seems to be literally

true . . . that she died because the flow of air was cut off. That's the end of it you might say. . . . From the medical point of view at least."

"Yes, but how did the air get cut off? It wouldn't take much sense to figure out that such a thing wouldn't happen of its own accord!" Anita smiled warmly as she said this.

"Of course you're right," Parks said. "But still these things are slippery. The doctor didn't rush right in and say he was sure she was choked to death by Rudy Peck! It seems hopeful somehow. . . ."

"And how was Peck during all this talk about the girl? That's a terrible thing to go through. And it was not actually the girl at all, not a real personality with all its complications. What this trial is about is the girl's body after death, what all the various people who saw this corpse have to say about it! Isn't that strange? It makes the whole thing unreal and yet more terrible, much more terrible. The character of the persons involved gets completely lost, buried under this pile of fact and description."

"We can't know now what these two people were like—" Parks said.

"Still, what everyone cares about is the two personalities, what they were like, what they thought of each other."

"It's too late now. One of them is dead and the other is on trial for murder. Their character as it was before has vanished. We'll never know whether she loved him or not. . . . That doesn't interest me much."

"But the markings on the body, the discoveries made at the morgue, those aren't the great thing either! Are you to discover and do justice to what the two were when both were alive or are you to conduct the trial for the dead one alone? That's the problem."

The chicken sandwich arrived and Anita quite suddenly turned all her attention to it in a way that surprised Parks. She ate it solemnly and quickly, hardly looking up, as if she were alone and very hungry. Carefully, curiously Parks watched her. He liked her long-fingered, knotty hands, her smooth face, sharp and noble, and yet somehow drooping, conscience-stricken, her wonderful eyes, that perfectionist glance, which seemed to be in revolt against the infirmity of her shy and haunted smile. At the collar of her dress, a black pleated woolen skirt and yellowish jersey top, she was wearing a small ornament of gold, a lizard with a red stone in its head.

"I spoke to Rudy's parents, to the Pecks," Parks said, speaking softly and elegiacally, forgetful of the noise and clatter in the diner. "I was compelled to do it somehow, even though I suppose the kindest thing would be to let them go their way unnoticed. . . . You know they drive back and forth from their home every day . . . quite a few miles from here, in an old car. I have seen them myself in the car. . . . It's unforgettable and yet you wish you hadn't seen it. One of those clear and pitiful tableaux, the kind the naturalistic artists used to do out here . . . bleak sunlight, sturdy faces, rugged landscape, and yet all very sad, melancholy as some abandoned beach. These people, the parents, are poor, simple, and good, that's the way they appear and I've heard nothing that would indicate otherwise. . . . When you see them you feel they represent the most profound question of the universe.

110

What do they mean? Why are they chosen for this torment? If you had to answer that question, or if you even tried to take it seriously I suppose you'd go mad. I don't believe these people even ask it themselves, or, if so, only rhetorically. They know there is no answer. . . . A stroke of lightning . . ."

"It's all very ugly," Anita mumbled, gazing at Parks with a mysterious skepticism.

Parks could not fathom that expression of doctrinal dispute on Anita's face. He went on. "I was very much interested in the doctors this morning. I mean over and above the case. As I sat there watching them I was thinking that it might have been my own father on the stand. He's a doctor and no doubt he's done this sort of thing himself. . . . Never thought to ask him before. . . ." Parks hesitated thoughtfully, his eyes on his coffee cup. "Yes, doctors do work hard. Their life is demanding, more than most professions nowadays. . . . But still there's work, what everyone does more or less, and then there's something else—working man's *work*. . . . You have only to take a look at Rudy Peck's father to know what sort of work *he* does. Amazing that it should show in so many small ways. Yes, just one glance reveals that he's been a working man most of his life, and even a photograph of the girl's father, Mr. Henderson, convinces you that he's not the same thing. These differences have nothing to do with handsomeness. . . . They are just a fact. . . . And it isn't a simple matter, a different way of dressing. . . . It's something in the faces, the hands, the stoop—"

"Our lives do mark us!" Anita said. "Now, tell me about your father. You said he was a doctor, but I'd like to know a little more. I'm always interested in people's families."

When Parks paused to consider this Anita added, "Of course, you're not Southern and perhaps you can't do much with the subject of families. My friend, Harold March, says that in the South you can just invent a family to please your fancy. People won't even insist upon the evidence of the eye, if you have the nerve to say otherwise."

"March?" Parks asked, sorry for the intrusion of a name new to him.

"He lives in our house, a lodger. Perhaps you know him, Harold March. He's in your department."

"As a matter of fact I do, vaguely, vaguely. . . . Well, I haven't the honor to be Southern but I do have a family."

Parks felt some conceit about his talent for bringing his father into faraway places, dropping the old man upon strangers in a lump, all formed and tagged and done up. He smiled. "My father . . . my father . . . let me see. He's not a man to be reduced to an epigram. Well, he enjoys himself thoroughly, by which I do not mean to suggest that he devotes himself to having a good time. No, he enjoys *being* himself. It's the consolation of his existence to take stock hourly and thank heaven he's not someone else. . . . You might think he'd be impossible feeling this way, but on the contrary it gives him a certain charm, a gladness that's quite original. . . . He brightens the room when he enters because he believes everyone is enchanted to see him again. . . . A doting mother behind all this, no doubt. . . . I can still see his flirtatious little smile, rather naïve and trusting. At breakfast in the morning he's superb, shaved, combed, brushed, and dressed, positively glowing with the pleasure his existence will give everyone who comes in his path. The thing I've always wondered about him, the main thing—does he really like people, this glowing, glad man? Not at all, I believe now. His grandness, his gaiety is a form of politeness to his adorers, he owes the worshipers that. He prides himself on never having had a friend borrow money from him—he gives them his charm instead. His own brother he dislikes heartily, detests him really, is always calling him a coward, and accuses him of 'oiling the machinery' and passing out cigars, as if that were a crime. All of this to-do over the brother began long ago, when the brother, Uncle Wilt, was elected to a higher office than my father in a club they both belonged to."

Anita followed this speech without any noticeable restlessness and Parks, an almost childlike enthusiasm gripping him now, went further. "My father, as I mentioned before, is a doctor, a bone surgeon. I think he is a very good one; everyone seems to think so. I must be just to him and say he takes his work very seriously and he seems very clever about all that, just as clever as he is obstinate about so many other things. We live in a suburb of New York City in a strange memorial to my father's interference and vanity, a Cape Cod and Southern Colonial mixture . . . very outlandish and quaint because my father was busy fascinating the architect and getting his own way. . . . Let's see, what else about him. He went to Dartmouth and so did I. . . ."

"Do you like your father?" Anita asked, with an inquisitive air.

Parks felt a bit suspicious of this question. "Like him? I suppose I do and yet he is not an ideal of mine, although of course he once was when I was quite young. It was really not until I went into the army that I fully realized some of the limitations of my father's point of view about things. His point of view and that of most of his friends. . . ."

"What did you learn in the Army?"

Parks had at this point the impression Anita was disappointed in him. He had an abnormally keen eye, like a Jesuit's, for a delinquent impulse. "I'm sure it wouldn't be the least bit interesting to you. I'm going on like a windbag—" His eyes wandered about the restaurant, which had now filled up with boys and girls in plum- and mustard-colored jackets who were attending a high-school basketball tournament.

"But I most certainly am interested," Anita said, hardly hiding her amusement.

"I'm sure you'll only laugh at me," Parks said jauntily. "It will sound too serious. You'll think I'm trying to make myself important—"

"Suppose you are. I'd still like to know what sort of change you think the Army made."

"The usual thing, nothing exceptional. You sometimes hear it called an 'enlargement of experience' and actually it was just that!" Parks recalled a Negro boy who stuttered, especially when he was standing alone and someone suddenly called out his name. By these recollections he hoped to give form to the pity, shame, and love aroused during the army years, to express his vision of injustice, the quickened conscience which had ennobled his life. Or, shifting the scene, he would say, "America hasn't been nearly democratic enough after the war. . . . It's a fantastic irony to find us supporting feudal systems in Europe, lining up with the Church and conservative coalitions of the center. . . ."

Parks, slumbering long, had, as he expressed it, "awakened." "The way a bird knocks off its shell and squeaks!" Coming suddenly into the state of enlightenment was thrilling but unsettling; he let himself go as a poor man will with a legacy, laying up in a tumble the necessary, the beautiful, and the vulgar. Parks hadn't any systematic notions, nor any dogmatic ideas about the improvement of the world. It was too late for him to be a Communist, an Agrarian, a Medievalist. Instead he was suffused with a sensitive, extraordinary decadence: his luxurious, genuine, heartfelt addiction to the pathetic, and perhaps this was in some special sense revolutionary. The pathetic included a great deal, almost every sad incongruity; it seeped into every corner like a fog. So Parks could condemn, with an utter absence of cynicism and deviousness, his country's aid to democratic countries after the war because it was also supporting reactionaries in Greece. But this was a mere sideline, because Parks was not deeply interested in politics. A personal deviation stirred him more than a national one; an abandoned child caused his moral being to cry out more quickly than an election, a *coup d'état*. His sovereign indignation blew around the world like a warm Gulf Stream wind, caressing the sad everywhere. This breeze had now touched Rudy Peck's cheek, the unfortunate creature, blighted but once blooming son of the poor. Parks's use of the word *poor* was highly creative and he could sometimes be heard lamenting, "Well, naturally poor people have only one automobile, and if the father has to use that for his work the son may feel a sense of deprivation because he hasn't a car to whiz his girl about in!" or again, "The *poor* go to the public swimming pools." Parks sometimes recognized the comedy of his definitions—he was diving for something real and could not always name it.

"What about your mother?" Anita asked, lighting a cigarette. "Do you get along with her?"

"My mother?" Parks said, hesitating. "She's a very nice woman, a very good sort. Naturally, she goes along with everything my father says, because she truly admires him. Still she's got her own character, her own instincts. . . . I think she might have had some fine career of her own if she had wished—"

At Parks's questioning, Anita gave a short description of herself, her husband, which did not at all satisfy Parks. He had no time to insist upon a fuller account because Anita relentlessly went on with her inquisition. "What do you mean to do with yourself?" she demanded.

"Oh, now you've touched a tender spot," Parks said with a somewhat forced bounciness. "It's not a fair thing to ask—as secret as my salary which doesn't exist. I've achieved absolutely nothing. . . . I've wasted a lot of time, on medical studies for instance, and I hadn't the slightest aptitude for them, nor interest even. Of course, I can't undo that and it might be worse. . . . I'm not as young as I ought to be and not too old either, I suppose. I admit I'm not the most confident man in the world. . . . The genius act seems a little dated, don't you think? . . .

116

Well, after these apologies I'll confess that I want to be a writer. How can I express it . . . I don't set any great store by myself and yet I have hopes. It's a bit embarrassing to try to explain."

"What will you write about? What have you been writing about, perhaps I should say?"

Parks replied that he didn't quite know and yet, on the other hand, he certainly did know too. Perhaps he would write about the boys in the army, or all the crippling things he had seen in his life, right in his town, in the summer on Long Island Sound. Little pockets of shameful sordidness, cruelty or indigence—the haunting Jewish family who ran the cigar store: their wonderful faces, parchment pale and crinkled, their heavy beautiful hair, mingled gray and black.

"But there's no lack of books about those things, we could hardly have more in my opinion," Anita said firmly. She was herself a great reader of popular novels and spoke sharply and with a toss of her head which meant that she knew whereof she spoke.

Parks's pride flickered brightly for a moment. "There are some good ones of course," he said heatedly. "But I wouldn't say there were too many. Naturally, there are probably no new subjects under the sun, entirely new ones. It is always the treatment that counts. If you look at popular novels and movies you'll see it's always the same old thing, false and unimaginative. A dressed-up, pink-and-white, sugary picture of America . . . the old tired romance where the poor girl marries the rich boy."

"Sometimes she *can* do that! People, even rich ones, have complicated and hidden motives that won't allow

117

them to be satisfied except in these odd ways, rich people marrying poor ones and the other way round."

Anita looked up at the clock. "I must go. I want to get into that damned trial this afternoon. I'd better arrive before everyone comes back from lunch." Standing up, hurrying, she thanked Parks with great warmth and was out of the restaurant before he could get his breath.

Alone, Parks began to regret his performance. What a paltry recitation, he thought, all that dragging in the old folks! He hadn't done them properly at all and they weren't "old folks." His parents had distressingly to be taken as contemporaries: his mother, a large woman who played golf and wore tailored suits, had her hair done once a week and touched up with a bit of silvery dye, who liked to go bathing in cold water in her white, sharkskin suit with a modest, wide skirt. And his father tall, lean, impressive in his gray flannel shorts on a Sunday morning.

In the witness box uneasy voices remembered. College girls in sweaters and pearls, their lips purplish, their faces dusted with rosy-brown powder, one handsome girl after another in pink or red or blue wool told what she had heard or seen. "Rudy appeared disturbed about something, unnaturally alarmed when Betty Jane was late, imagining she was out with another boy."

And, "Yes, she spoke of him, sir, of Rudy. Yes, that night I was with her. She said she wanted to be friendly with him, that she liked him, but was no longer in love with him. That's the way she put it."

And flatly, "Betty Jane was always a happy person. Always laughing, always had a joke."

Another said, "I certainly never got the idea she was engaged to Rudy, that she meant it *that* seriously. She never said anything to me about being ready to get married, or even wanting to."

One girl, sharp-chinned with clipped, shining red hair hugging her head tightly, flat against her cheekbone and forehead, a profile on a coin, yellowish eyes staring deeply into the prosecutor's gray ones, this one remarked bluntly, "Betty Jane said at the time to me, on the night I'm talking about, that Rudy was distasteful to her. Distasteful is

119

the word she used!" These sentences came out, rat-tat-tat, like the sound of a gun, each little bullet-word clicking out one by one.

The boy's nostrils flared in anguish. His gaze seemed to be transfixed by the gleam of tortoise-shell barrettes on the girls' hair or shifting he would stare painfully at the classroom notebooks in their laps. These witnesses apparently bore him no ill will. They spoke of Rudy and Betty Jane with familiarity as if the girl were still alive and Rudy still a face on the campus in a sweater and topcoat, or standing in the corner of the drawing room at the sorority house at teatime, talking idly. The girls did not acknowledge that at present he had no existence, was on his way either to death or to a merciless rebirth. Their simplicity was a more dreadful and searing thing than all the professionalism of the court, all the machinery of the law which passed him along, here and there, as if he were a package not yet claimed. Those bright voices spoke from the lost Eden and he heard them from the gates.

The rebuttal: "Yes, I think she did have further dates with him after the statement she made. I don't know for certain whether she broke off with him entirely or not."

And: "No, she didn't exactly show her distaste in *all* her actions, only sometimes. I don't know whether that is a contradiction or not, sir. I don't think she went out of her way to see Rudy, but at the same time she didn't seem to want to hurt his feelings."

Or: "Yes, as I recall she did take his arm that night. I think she did. I'm not certain. Yes, the same night when she said she liked him but wasn't in love with him."

Betty Jane's soul contained multitudes. There she was

late at night, in the morning, at the coffee shop, walking in the snow, at the movies—sharp, white-toothed smile, delicate, fair face—and, oh, the moodiness of sunny natures, those unaccountable statements and retractions.

No one could imagine what Rudy was thinking when he saw these friends from the past, these girls of his own age, some laconic, others simply capable with tranquil bodies and intelligent eyes, and all clearly glad when they could step out of the witness box.

Among the crowd some old heads nodded, sleepy with the glare of buff-tinted walls. Plain, red-cheeked, wrinkled faces drooped uncontrollably, having an afternoon nap. The very difficulty of discovering Betty Jane's nature caused some to yawn from the effort. In the lobby outside the courtroom, boys in blue-green trousers and girls in snow boots and bare legs wandered about, talking, waiting, listening with indeterminate expressions. It was impossible to guess partisanship, to say who among their contemporaries most regretted Betty Jane or worried for Rudy.

Anita disliked the girls on the witness stand. She was vexed by their smooth brows, their artless serenity before the mighty course of human life, their sweet lack of wonder at the crashing stars. Even their effort, as pure and fabulous as a philosopher's, to state the exact truth of their scanty reminiscences seemed to her a grim joke nature plays on the young, leading it to believe nothing will be denied the strong will. In all this there was an amateurish recklessness which made her blood run cold: what was to be hoped for Rudy, what would become of him, his very life, if all this chatter of love and happiness was to settle it. She winced when they said "happy" or "in love" or "not in love." Was Rudy to be condemned if it could be proved the girl did not love him, thereby giving him a motive for violence? Love! The emotion the deepest persons believed to be nonexistent except by the side of a certain measure of hatred.

On the stand another witness searched this abyss of feeling. "I'd say myself they were fond of each other from the looks of it. They were always together it seemed to me, and nearly always laughing and having a good time. I joked myself with this girl about the boy and she just smiled."

"Idiots!" Anita was thinking. Of course, of course, they loved and hated each other, they were together and apart, bound and free. They couldn't come to terms, these ruined egoists who thought they were meant to be happy, to love and be loved by just the right person. These thoughts drifted through Anita's mind, bothering her like an illness. The nakedness of the question, which challenged without a tremble the very meaning of life.

Furiously Anita imagined the spectators and the jury turning over the deadly mystery, weighing the secret desire. If she didn't *like* him, why was she always seeing him? Or if she did truly care for him, why was she always telling her girl friends she didn't have serious feelings on the matter? If she preferred other young men, why was she often with this one? But if she was in love with this one, why had so many of her friends heard her say she was not? These questions circled about like a hungry bird, beating the air, hovering, flapping furiously, on and on in a dizzy flight without destination.

What Anita wanted said was quite the opposite. She felt the jury ought to be instructed that each day for almost everyone in the world was a capitulation at some point, a sore compromise—that was the best of it, the best one could hope. At the worst, like this case, one clearly saw something more complex, but not at all unusual or unexpected. Universal psychic lesions made people do what they did not entirely wish to do and, consonantly, prevented them from completely and thoroughly wanting the happiness they superficially pursued. It seemed clear that this boy and girl both liked and disliked each other. What was the need of pretending an absolute? It was unjust for Rudy to have to carry such an impossible demand on his back. Still, she felt the college girls acted and spoke as if they believed the absolutes, as if they were sure to find them in their own lives. How she wearied of those creaseless faces and fresh eyes, their repetitive vocabularies, their jazzy little certainties, their want of knowledge about life. It wore her down to the bone and made her want to cry.

Dreamily she floated off from this unpleasing parade of untroubled youth, this unwholesome trustfulness. She slipped back into her own younger days, those years of hard shocks and smarting wounds which still fretted her nerves but which she never tired of thinking about. She returned to them as a child returns to the scab on his knee, picking it off so that the wound might fester anew. Indeed her own experience seemed to her to have an annihilating uniqueness and obstinacy, even though the scene had been set and the characters assembled a million times before, as she well knew. But what she found so original in her own drama was the formlessness, the fascinating lack of expected shape. All contraries could easily be true of her youth, she thought.

Perhaps she had *really* loved her mother after all and if so what a joke that was on her because she thought she had hated her mother, had resented her almost to the point of madness. But no, perhaps it was not that she had truly loved her mother, but that she had only pretended to care for her father, to sympathize with him, falling in this instance deeply into filial hypocrisy. Some emotional law seemed to demand that one love at least one of his parents, but perhaps she had scorned both of them, acknowledging the law only by her counterfeit of feeling for her father. But what a dreadful thing to admit, a spirit of ice at only nine years old!

Anita had no difficulty recalling her mother's image. The old lady seemed always to be just around the corner, an unchanging reality in the same figured rayon dress piped with black at the neck. Their dim parlor with its great, purplish overstuffed chair nearly bald from much brushing lived on into eternity, detailed and fixed. Her mother's usual nature had been quiet, a sickly *pianissimo*, and always inhospitable because she was overcome with nerves and migraine after a visit of any length, an occurrence of any crude force, a dog sniffing at the flower beds. But nevertheless this lady was not limited in her charity, the grotesque charity of a cripple trying to dance in behalf of orphans—ill and in pain Anita's mother was nearly always ready to do several quiet hours in the evening at the bedside of a sick neighbor, scorning pay, gratitude, even a fresh pot of tea during the vigil. Yes, ordinarily a boring monotonous woman, short on conversation and temperament, neither happy in her present life nor able to recall a chance for glory missed in the past, an offer foolishly turned down, a path beckoning and unheeded. She seemed like her image and her parlor to have been where she was forever, was unimaginable any place else or in other circumstances, a work of immutable portraiture, colored and placed long ago. And yet the statue spoke, declaimed in fact, with unnerving regularity and vigor. Once every three weeks or so the wife would greet her husband, Anita's father, with what could accurately be called a "cyclone of abuse," a circular ill wind of words, speedy and destructive. He never knew when to expect it, but it blew up before the month was out certainly, waited for him when he came home in the evening from his bicycle shop, for such was the father's livelihood and passion, new bicycles, in the old days from England, or tinkering with the broken spokes of damaged ones. Even the noise she made herself was painful to her and so Anita's mother would speak rather softly when the evil mood came upon her, but rapidly, firmly, and interminably, relishing repetition. She went on at the man fantastically until the seizure was over. The accusation, coughed out in the gloom, was that Anita's father could hardly be spoken of as a man at all and certainly bore no relation to any ideal. He was a soft-headed, mushy creature, a coward with an expression as sweet as St. Sebastian's when the arrows hit, or sometimes a tail-wagging cur, whimpering, yapping at the heels of his own betrayer. All of this had its origin in an unfortunate partnership, one of those stumbling business affairs of the past, a union which seemed to Anita to have taken place in the dawn of time.

In this unlucky instance, Anita's father had not only lost his money through unwise investment but had actually been tricked out of the sum of several thousand dollars by a dishonest partner. The embarrassed man had been able to do nothing except apologize to his wife, who did not blame the thieving partner but blamed the robbed one. From that time the tirades dated and in the midst of them the father was just as helpless as he had been with the thief. He looked rightly accused and filled with manly regret for all his sad wife had endured at his hands.

These dark, ravaging quarrels were unbearable to Anita. She shrank timidly from them and yet she felt a most powerful bitterness, a fierce resentment and thought she had got a worse break in life than an orphan. She could not discover the slightest element of comedy in her parents, as she saw others able to do. Their cramped absurdity was understood to the full by the daughter. Very early she was able to see their faults as clearly as if they were her neighbors and not her own flesh and blood. She was morbidly sensitive about them and would have exchanged them had it been possible. "But I am not a lost princess, I am theirs!" she reminded herself always.

In her youth nearly everyone she met had seemed to her luckier than herself. She had envied so many people and at the same time had despaired of having any accidental, undeserved good luck come her way or of making anything desirable by her own efforts. How awful to remember that envy, that horrible, sniveling envy of adolescence which could attach itself to anything—to a painted porch swing, a mother with red, curly hair, the gift of tap dancing. Her thoughts were filled with clear, brutal questions.

126

How could she be other than she was with these two people behind her, this couple who at their best attained no
greater heights than the worthy dullness and spiritless de-
pendability of good domestics. Her mother's rages were
a backstairs secret, more depressing than her calm, but
with their lack of variety not even vividly dramatic. What
was there to joke about or pass off with cleverness in twenty-three years of this desert, twenty-three years of those
evening meals at which her mother folded her hands and
said grace and then led them off to some truncated, monotonous, faltering repartee—this on what they called a "good
evening."

Now that she was older a measure of insight replaced
the old discontent. "They said grace at the table and went
to church but they weren't even religious, really!" Anita
said to her husband. "I can't even make them into one of
those seedy, evangelical couples!" She longed to reach a
final verdict, to assign the psychological blame for their
starved lives. But this verdict was not easy to arrive at
and she was dissatisfied with her own interpretations.
Her mother had been too dominating, she would decide.
This domination and disappointment had drained her
father of his vanity and ambition, leaving him with that
fatal dryness worse than poverty. How clear it all was, and
yet couldn't it be that her father had been too passive,
too weak and pacific always and the discovery of these
disabilities had soured her mother's love. Still, she was
not even sure that her mother did not greatly love her
father. Even with the tirades, this remained a possibility
for that irregular personality, her mother. For herself,
Anita, the most fascinating subject of all, a thousand ques-

127

tions remained unanswered. Was she still tormented by her parents' inadequacy? How much, how much? Perhaps it was her own shrunken nature she lamented in the name of her parents. Did *they* make her uncomfortable when she went to a party, accompanying her along the way? Was it their dullness that made her inarticulate, fearing to be commonplace and monotonous herself? A lot of damage had been done and to know this was a consolation she wished to offer everyone.

"Psychology" had come to Anita like a fascinating rumor. She held it to her heart as one would a profitable idea of one's own, a lucky intuition. Sometimes she went to the library and took out books on this subject, but study was not necessary. These great new ideas circled about the air and one had only to breathe deeply to take them in, this great liberating air. For some reason she did not like the actual reading of Freud: that austere magician seemed to her to go too far, to leave her behind from the start. He was, she admitted, the very god of the springtime of this immense new world, but he frightened her, just as the great Assyrian sculptures in a museum had once filled her with unpleasant shudders, a feeling of numbness and littleness.

Anita was ordinarily indifferent to public events, but she had become infatuated with Rudy's case from the very moment she first read about it in the newspapers. Immediately, without waiting for the story's peculiar circumstances, those unsettling second thoughts, she saw him as a sacrificial animal, the fresh young lamb to be offered up for society's well-being. She could hardly think, without an ache of despair for mankind, of his abasement, his

128

dangerous situation, which was that of a mythical youth who could turn neither to the left nor the right. Superstition, sentimentality—these meant to have their way with Rudy Peck. Dismally, nervously, her mind returned again and again to the notion that Betty Jane Henderson had in the deepest sense brought about her own death, longed for it, insisted upon it, driven Rudy Peck to achieve it. There was a sickening, witch-burning pedantry that meant to punish the boy for what in the profoundest truth was not his responsibility.

Just how all this had come about Anita was not prepared to say. Alas, she knew neither of the principals personally and in a such a case that was the only knowledge to be trusted. But she felt in her bones, in her very life's blood, the tragic destiny of the personal existence. To see the weak, struggling, helplessly human suddenly reduced to the cold and legal, to mere concept, to consequence, was in this case more than she could bear. Not legally, but humanly Betty Jane Henderson had provoked her own destruction. This was not an accidental meeting of a murderer and his unknown victim. No, these matters took two, she would repeat again and again. They take time, time rusting the surface like dripping water.

Anita was convinced that Rudy was *good*. Now after the cleansing by fire he must be purer than he had been before. She *knew*, she saw it in his face, this existence broken into pieces, scattered and then in suffering put together again. It was her belief people could achieve their best selves only after some agonizing face-to-face meeting with their worst, after they had met in darkness the unutterable green, shining face of confusion, desire, and dis-

129

tortion—and found, screaming, this image to be their own. No, Rudy was not a murderer. Perhaps he had not in any way harmed Betty Jane, but *if he had, if he had,* the psychological truth was that Betty Jane had come at him with a knife, a weapon more powerful for not being actual. Somehow she threatened, struck at his very being, and he had killed her in self-defense, in every way the defense of the *self* and not only of his body.

Just yesterday Harold March had said to Anita, "Leniency has come upon you like a seizure. It seems to be as unsettling as revenge." George, her husband, laughed and picked up an almond.

The trial was resumed. The witness now appearing was the subject of some controversy, Rudy's side wishing him to be declared ineligible, the State pressing strongly for his admission. After a lengthy deliberation with his books and precedents, his conscience, legal and moral, the judge decided to subpoena the testimony of the college psychologist. This person held an academic degree rather than a medical one and therefore was not necessarily included among those who may plead inviolable confidence. The psychologist, Dr. Elmer Ashton, had asked to be released from testifying and when this was not granted he expressed his regret, saying he believed the decision arrived at would handicap him in his work of student counseling.

Anita saw before her in the witness box a youthful, round, heavy face with an almost flattened nose, strong chin, full cheeks, blue eyes, light hair worn short in the

Prussian manner, relaxed shoulders in a cashmere sweater and old jacket of good cut. All of this added up in her view to a brilliant patrician homeliness. When he pronounced his name, Dr. Ashton spoke in a soft-voweled accent, resembling the Southern but in fact the accent of a private school in the East. The absence of the intransigent Iowa consonants cheered Anita's heart, which had a little snobbishness in it and an exceptional imagination, since she had herself only known the world of the central and western states. In this respect, she retained some of the poetic gift and dreaminess of the old pioneers who could see the horizon beyond the mud flats.

"What is this unusual man doing *here?*" she wondered, thinking of him as a consolation, a discovery, although she would not have presumed to try to know him. Already Dr. Ashton sparkled with excellence and glowed with talent, those two qualities Anita worshiped. She admired his manly, short fingers as he touched his collar for a moment, waiting for the questions. She liked his smile, his old jacket with suède patches on the elbows. He seemed to her to come from the new world, to bring a glorious message.

"Now, Doctor Ashton, if that's the right way to address you—" Mr. Garr began.

"Mister is sufficient, sir."

"Well, Doctor, if you don't mind. Is it true that you had a conversation with Mr. Peck, the defendant, several months previous to Miss Betty Jane Henderson's death?"

"Yes, yes, that is true."

"Now, did this person, Mr. Peck, feel some urgency

about the conversation? Had he consulted you in your professional capacity, privately and seriously?"

"Yes, I think it would be accurate to agree to that."

"Now, will you tell the court the content of the conversations last September, give them an account of the boy's reason for wanting to see you?"

Dr. Ashton rubbed his chin thoughtfully, not answering immediately. His merciful and unsurprised gaze wandered about the courtroom, resting at last on the wall behind the jury box.

"The content, the general content, you mean?" he said finally.

"Yes. Why did he come to see you, please?"

"Mr. Peck came to see me in September. He said he was troubled by feelings of anxiety."

"I believe these feelings of anxiety were more concrete, were they not, Doctor Ashton?" Mr. Garr pursued warily. "Will you tell the court to the best of your recollection what this young man was feeling anxious about last September?"

"Yes. He expressed anxiety over impulses to take his own life and also to assault murderously the girl he was going with. He was alarmed. He said he was in love, astonished and troubled by these impulses."

"Did Rudy Peck indicate any reason for these feelings, any motive or background to them?"

"No, he did not."

"Has it been your experience, Doctor, that these feelings of violence are usually caused by jealousy, great fear of losing a loved one to another?" Mr. Garr insisted.

"Sometimes they are," Dr. Ashton agreed with a nod. "I have observed that upon occasion."

"Was it your impression that jealousy played a part in this instance? Did the young man mention Betty Jane Henderson?"

"Not by name. He referred only to the girl he was in love with."

"Did you ask Mr. Peck if he had jealous emotions about the girl he was in love with?"

"Yes, I did, and he denied being jealous of her with respect to any other man."

Mr. Garr sighed. "Now, sir," he said rapidly, "will you tell the jury when Mr. Peck first told you of his destructive impulses?"

"In September of last year. He telephoned me at three-thirty in the morning."

"What was his condition, in your opinion?"

"He was troubled. He said he had the desire to throw himself under a truck."

"After your interview what course did you advise?"

"I made an appointment with a psychiatrist for the soonest time possible. It is my belief that Mr. Peck did not keep the appointment."

Dr. Ashton coughed, rubbed his chin again, calmly thinking. Anita watched the faces of the jurors. It was now late on in the afternoon and the room was over-heated. Anita felt defeated in the hope that her own subtle appreciation, so quick and discriminating, would also be shared by the jurors. Dr. Ashton's testimony was of overwhelming complexity. Separated from voice and gesture, from that contemplating glance and warm under-

133

standing, what the psychologist had actually said perhaps condemned Rudy. The headlines could easily be foreseen now that Anita had a bit of practice with the discrepancy between her own impressions and the report of the press. TOLD DOCTOR WANTED TO KILL GIRL! That was true, but couldn't the jury see something beyond this in what the doctor said? The answer lay in the doctor himself, in his calm, humane pronouncing of the damaging words, in the way he seemed to indicate that such emotions were not of great rarity in his work, that Rudy was neither the first nor the last to come to him with such fears.

Turning about slowly, searching the faces, Anita was not encouraged. "Can it all be wasted?" she asked, despairing. True, the jurors were looking at the psychologist with amazed eagerness, taking in his cropped head, listening in the warm afternoon to that conversation of some months ago. Do they perhaps think Rudy should have been put in jail *then?* What would they have done? Called the police, most likely.

Mr. Garr bowed politely to the psychologist and turned him over to Rudy's lawyer, Mr. Brice. Mr. Brice smiled at the doctor in a comradely way, taking upon himself some of the grace bestowed by the man's impersonal benevolence. Anita was delighted with Mr. Brice, the way he had of bending forward, speaking humbly when it was useful. She was impressed by the ability of these small-town lawyers, their brilliance even, something she would never have dreamed without the trial. Virtuosity was apparently hidden everywhere and could be summoned when the occasion demanded.

Mr. Brice looked at a small card upon which he had

been writing. "Was this boy, Rudy, distraught when he came to see you?"

"No, he was not distraught. He said he was troubled and apparently he was, but he was certainly not distraught in appearance."

"And you say he consulted you about impulses of suicide?"

"Yes, he did."

"And homicidal impulses, is that correct?"

"That is correct."

Mr. Brice paused again, looking out of the window beyond. "Would you say that Rudy's consulting you about these impulses showed an aversion to them?"

Dr. Ashton considered for a moment. "Yes, I believe it might be interpreted in that way. I think one could accurately assume that if it were otherwise he would not have consulted me."

"Do you think there might in such an example be a little self-dramatization, not to be taken too seriously, something we have all experienced in ourselves and in others?"

"I can say that self-dramatization is sometimes a factor in these matters. Whether or not it existed in this particular case I couldn't judge because of the inadequate number of consultations."

"In your opinion, Rudy expressed complete rejection of these notions?"

"Complete rejection? I wouldn't and didn't phrase it that way."

"I beg your pardon, Doctor. How would you describe his mood about these impulses?"

135

"He was troubled about them."

"Troubled enough to consult you?"

"Yes, sir, that is true."

Rudy's lawyer moved nearer the witness box. "Now, Doctor Ashton, if you chose a hundred people, let us say . . . just any hundred from an average group of citizens . . . wouldn't seventy-five per cent of them have had, at one time or another, suicidal and homicidal impulses?"

Dr. Ashton sniffed slightly and pondered without hurry. "I think I have read that seventy per cent of a group questioned in the Navy admitted having had suicidal impulses at some time in their lives. About homicidal impulses, I haven't any figures at hand."

"Have you received the impression in your study and your work that many people have homicidal impulses at one time or another in their lives, that these are normal and not to be taken too seriously in most instances?"

"I wouldn't wish to answer that without great qualification and at some length."

"Thank you, Doctor," Mr. Brice said breezily.

Mr. Garr returned to the witness, not willing to let things stand as they were. "Doctor," he said primly, "would you agree with the commonly accepted observation that jealousy is frequently a motive for homicidal impulses?"

Dr. Ashton acquiesced in the possibility of there being some truth in the common experience and retired from the stands, followed by Anita's passionate eyes.

During the short recess Anita remained in her seat, not going out into the lobby even though she was thirsty. Lazily she thought of Parks, trying to describe and define

136

his personality. "This is a new wrinkle," she thought, "this wishing to be lowly and feeling sorry you haven't been unjustly persecuted." She didn't for a moment believe in it, was suspicious of its authenticity and hostile to its reckless simplicity. She did not see that Parks had any occasion for self-reproach in this grand manner. He's not a titan of privilege nor a king of oppression! she concluded. In her view Parks was usurping a throne not truly his in quite the same way some wretched madman imagined himself to be Napoleon. Where did he get all this guilt? she wondered. It seemed one only had to have a happy life to abdicate all his rights in a fit of self-denial.

Had Anita been acquainted with the town gossip she might have been expecting the next witness for the prosecution, since the tale that was to come had spread all over town in many versions. Instead, she was taken by surprise when she saw a woman in her late thirties advance sheepishly into the drama, taking one uncertain step after another but at last landing firmly on the witness seat and surveying the crowd with a friendly little nod and an artless grin. This witness had a vacant brown face, full lips, and short teeth of a chalky appearance. She was not unattractive, but rather childishly dim and yielding, with a provisional air about her, as though her whole character were subject to revision on a moment's notice. The woman was wearing a small brown hat with a swing of fringe on one side and on the other the fringe of her own brown-gray hair. She was pleasantly attired in a suit of soft material, rosy-and-green-hued like heather, and decorated with many buttons of mixed shades, agate bright. Her shifting smile flashed weakly, sweet-natured and scared. This roving, unsteady smile fell briefly upon Rudy. He thrust his shoulders back and stared coldly and stiffly at the woman, who blinked, showing surprise.

Her name was Mrs. Maisie Finch, she said, commanding as well as she could a voice as straying and fitful as her glance.

"Are you acquainted with the defendant, Mr. Rudolph Peck?" Mr. Garr asked in a shepherding voice.

"Oh, yes, I know *him*," Mrs. Finch said, looking at Rudy again with a cordial eye.

They had worked in the same restaurant that very fall. She supposed three months together, he as a waiter and she as a pastry cook in the morning and the salad-maker for the dinner hour. Helplessly, as if her eyes returned without control to this face she knew, she stared at the accused, Rudy, with a proprietary, cow-soft kitchen warmth, her unfinished countenance pleading something not expressible by her appearance in court. "I can't help it! They got me here!" the pleading smile seemed to say.

With genuine fondness she pronounced the name of the restaurant where she was still employed just as in the days when Rudy was there. The name fell from her lips with a loving cadence, spoken by one with many memories and pleasant recollections. She took joy, that one saw, in the University teachers and students, the joy of an old, devoted janitoress. And her kitchen, where the boys came and went, working their way, the mere mention of her duties in this place was like the castle memories of ancient servants.

138

"Mrs. Finch," Mr. Garr said with unusual rapidity, "did you have occasion to speak to the defendant, this young fellow here, about the girl named Betty Jane Henderson?"

"He spoke to me on his own, if that's what you mean. I didn't ask him anything without his starting first!"

"He spoke to you, you say. Can you recall when this was?"

"Just when school started. Last week of September most likely. Maybe the first week in October . . . around there. . . ."

Mr. Garr pushed her toward the substance of the conversation. "Mrs. Finch, please tell the court, for the benefit of the jury, what Rudy Peck said to you."

"Well, he said to me, Rudy did, I mean . . . he said that he had wanted to kill the girl that past summer somewhere. . . ."

"Somewhere?" Mr. Garr said, frowning.

"I can't remember just what place he mentioned, but it was someplace where they both were at the time. . . . He went there to see her. . . . Maybe it was another state, I've forgotten by now. Anyway, he said he wanted to kill her then but couldn't bring himself to."

"What did you say when you heard this?"

"I thought sure he was kidding, just as anyone would think about such a thing. I joshed him about it and he said no, he was serious. That's what he said."

"Thank you, madame," Mr. Garr said in a melancholy way.

While Mrs. Finch was testifying, Rudy shook his head violently for everyone to see, furiously denying the words, the sentences as they appeared. Mrs. Finch observed this negating activity with bewilderment. She looked at Rudy, blinked dangerously, as if she might weep.

Mr. Brice approached the witness jauntily, his lightness discounting her performance.

"Mrs. Finch. Now, just where was it Rudy said he was when he meant to kill the girl?"

"I can't remember, just as I told the other man here. He just mentioned the name of the place once where he had had the idea to do it."

"Very well. You don't remember the place, but you do remember the rest of his statement, remember every word?"

"Every word? I don't know about that, but I certainly do remember what he said and he said what I've just told you."

"Why is your recollection about this so much more certain than your recollection about the place?"

Mrs. Finch tossed her head proudly. "No, sir, I can't remember the place," she said with dignity, the brown fringe swaying, "but it was this other's being so queer that made me remember it!"

"Did he mention the girl's name?"

"No, he just said 'my girl.' At least that's what I think."

"Mrs. Finch," Mr. Brice said tenderly, "why do you think Rudy would tell *you* this? Did he say why he had chosen you as his confidante?"

"No, he didn't. And I sure wish he hadn't told me!"

Mr. Brice nodded in a kindly fashion and did not bother to question further, letting Mrs. Finch go on her way with no more blows from his cross-examination. Nervously, Mrs. Finch left the stand, looking about her with damp eyes, and yet her short body bristling with outraged dignity.

Anita left the courthouse soon after this when the trial adjourned for the day. Behind her someone said, "That Finch was a little peculiar, but would she say it if it wasn't true? Can you imagine someone making it up for nothing?"

"I'm not saying this one did, but people have been known to make up things in murder cases," another voice observed.

"He's done for, done for!" Anita cried, walking out into the wind with her coat unbuttoned and taking no notice of the cold.

A hurricane wind roared round the state in the evening, coming up with a suddenness and violence usual in this climate, providing once more that day-to-day knowledge of extremity which made the people so imperturbably cheerful. These tremendous humid heats and slushy, damp cold spells bred a bone immunity to the petulant nature of those who lived in moderate climates and felt affronted by an occasional rainy day or an unseasonable temperature. The hurricane was a glorious diversion unfortunately wasteful, or so a transient might say amidst the blowing, banging, and excitement.

Doris Parks sat at the kitchen table typing a letter to her mother. In her search for content there were many pauses, during which she scratched the table's yellow peeling paint with her fingernail. Doris had none of the common difficulties with her parents: she would no more have thought of fearing them than of squealing at the sight of a mouse. The truth was that her parents rather feared her. Their parental love was solidly grounded upon respect, a tender and somewhat perplexing respect which made them long and strive to be worthy of this candid, reasonable, gay, and generous daughter. Doris knew they credited her with a beautiful if sometimes disturbing *decency,* a trait her parents admired even when they found themselves unequal to their daughter's fair-mindedness and openness. They would sometimes gaze at her with a biting smile as she rose without effort above the spiritual dramas which tempted others to self-interested, hypocritical behavior.

Doris's mother, notably kind and forthright, could not overcome attitudes of excessive deference toward their rich old neighbor with an antique Rolls-Royce and two Italian gardeners—she simply could not help something unusually warm and polite happening to her smile when she passed the old lady in her garden. She would say to herself, "But she's an awfully nice woman," and then, pushing honesty further, "No, perhaps not really nice, but then she's very old, actually quite old."

And Doris's father: his blood ran cold when he thought of the national debt. He could not for the life of him believe this national debt to be entirely different from a private one and when he shuddered it was as if he himself had gone into a stupendous bankruptcy. All the New Deal economists in the world could not have talked away that shiver, which seemed to him to derive from the most elementary evidence of the senses.

Doris, her mother admitted with genuine interest, hardly seemed to see their rich old neighbor's exquisite gardens and shining, silver-fitted motorcar. No sense of the fascinating, humbling grandeur of these attainments swept through her. And yet the ears of this child, uncanny organs, could pick up from afar a bored sigh by the chauffeur or an oath from the gardeners. Her father, dogmatic and firm with men of his own age, somehow felt that

Doris's brilliant, careless grin when he talked of the "impossibility of carrying the whole world on our backs" was an act of confidence and optimism which made his sour train conversations with his like-minded friends seem contrary to the Christian spirit. He had suffered more than Doris because he had in his youth been almost poor and yet he felt he must guard against the meanness and self-righteousness of the "self-made man," at least in the presence of his daughter. By this phrase, Doris did not mean to celebrate the man of inherited wealth so much as the "unmade man" he would say with a laugh, not quite confident. Yes, Doris was adored by her parents, even though they confined themselves to restrained and commonsense expression of their emotion.

Although never an eager correspondent, Doris found that since she had married and come to Iowa communication with her parents was becoming unaccountably onerous. This came from a simple circumstance: she was struck dumb because she hadn't anything to say for herself. Nothing exceptional, nor even admirable. She had thought it interesting and somehow commendable being in Iowa in the first place, but she had already used *that*.

How long these Iowa afternoons were, how amazingly long! These hours were a cloud that would not lift—the drizzly chill of a mild attack of melancholy had touched Doris for the first time.

What to do? There were floor-waxing, sewing, painting furniture, cutting out recipes from the newspapers and pasting them into notebooks: unthinkable occupations for a girl with a serious nature. "These things are as sad as paper flowers," Doris would think as she climbed the steps to her third-floor flat, passing her neighbors' kitchens on the stairway, looking at the red-and-white cans labeled for flour, salt, and sugar, the indexed cookbooks wrapped in cellophane, Dutch kitchen clocks, shelves lined with flowered oilcloth. A peasant's kitchen with large copper pans and wooden bowls, a huge old blazing stove such as she saw in her imagination, these had some greatness and beauty. It was another thing to be mistress of a little efficiency pantry fit for a doll's house.

Or she might work, as many of the other young girls did, in insignificant jobs of secretarial and office work to help their student husbands. Bright, well-educated, once-pampered girls, who made fun of the office staff when they came home at night, cooked onion soup and made green salad with garlic dressing, all set out on a plain oaken table with straw mats and salt and pepper shakers of severe modern design. Of course these were the young wives Doris liked best, but recently even these girls, so like herself, filled her with dissatisfaction. There are so many of us! she said. And at times when she thought of these girls sitting down one night a week to try to write a poem or a short story she felt like weeping.

Doris was more racy and untamed than these wives, and on the other hand more conservative. She was not literary; she had not that vague, fearful, sustaining hope of talent and recognition. What Doris wanted was that her life should be interesting, not that she should be aware in stinging solitude and obscurity of the fineness of her perceptions, the immensity of her sensibility. One of her vanities was that she knew her own generation thoroughly

—she was sure when she looked about her that she understood exactly what people her own age were about. Their marriages fascinated her particularly. In her secret heart she was proud of having done an unusual thing in marrying Joe since they were in every way equals. They came from the same part of the country, they had a wedding very much like their parents had had: everyone was content. When her parents wrote, "Give our love to Joseph," and his parents addressed "our darling Doris"— they meant it! And what a stunning situation that was! She had cleverly rebelled against her friends by returning to this simple principle. She did not feel sorry for her husband and was therefore able to criticize him in a comfortable way which she would not have liked to forego.

Still Doris's life was not at all interesting and her indolence was not the marvelous old thing it had once been to her. She liked to laugh as much as ever, smoke cigarettes, drink cheap red wine, talk about the movies, the problems of minorities, the difficulties of being a painter in America. But she was young; she had not been shaped simply by her parents and relations, by poverty or wealth. She had *ideas,* she spent a great deal of time comparing her generation with preceding ones. "No," she would reflect, "we aren't like the people of the twenties or thirties either. . . . For one thing *we* don't drink quite as much, a lot less in fact. . . . We marry younger, or so people say, and have children earlier and more often. . . . Of course, there's a reason for that. An unmarried girl of thirty would appear very neurotic, a lesbian or something! . . . It was a lot easier when you were allowed to be waiting for the right man or suffering from disappointment. . . ."

Doris was in many ways already tired of her generation and wanted to make her own emendations, but she did not know just what these might be. And while she was waiting to do something outstanding, she had suddenly without a warning of any kind fallen into a hideous pit of idleness. She did not relish this word, she approached it cautiously, wondering how it was different from the "leisure" she would have been delighted to give the whole world had it been in her power to make such a gift. This great idea, leisure, had always appeared to her as a box of priceless, glittering jewels: books, music, painting, were the precious gems lying there for the fortunate persons. However, she had made horrid discoveries. Reading turned out to be for her a sometimes stultifying pleasure, like even the best chocolates in excess. She understood now the vapidity of those old, lonely Southern ladies who lay on the couch and read several novels a day. And their tinny little phonograph which perched on the dining table —even the swell of music began to annoy her restless mind.

This darkness which had fallen upon her, the awful pinch and pain as one day passed and another just like it began was the first truly dreadful experience of Doris's life. Before this there had always been a unity in her character, but now when she unexpectedly saw her face in a mirror, noted how fresh and lively it appeared, she was puzzled by this same old face which remained even when one was breaking into pieces.

Doris was glad that her husband was preoccupied with Rudy Peck's trial. Curious as she ordinarily was she made no effort to attend the trial and did not even always listen

147

attentively to Joe's accounts in the evening. When she thought of the trial it seemed to her too immense to be looked at. "The only way is for him to make a confession of some sort. An act of repentance of one kind or another," she said vaguely.

"What on earth are you talking about?" Parks said, astounded. "You aren't allowed to make confessions, repentances, as you so casually call them, in a trial for murder. For that, my little dove, you can get the electric chair! You certainly don't want that, do you? It seems a heavy price to pay for a gesture!"

"Of course, I don't want him strung up!" Doris said with confusion. ". . . I guess it is taken for granted that one can plead not guilty no matter what the truth is. . . . Is it immoral to plead not guilty even if it's not true?"

"I don't know. I think you're allowed to look at every circumstance in the light most favorable to yourself. . . . I mean you're allowed to do that ethically."

"I think it's a terrible burden to have to tell lies. Suppose he did kill the girl, but didn't at all want to, was truly horrified later, truly filled with regret and remorse and sorrow. With all that to weigh on you, it seems unbearable to have to add a lot of little lies simply to make a case, the pretense that goes on in a legal trial. . . . It's too much. . . . I should think anyone would be corrupted after that, ruined by not being able to make a real and decent account of his feelings, tell what happened. To bring his own regret into the open . . . repentance . . ."

"Repentance?" Parks said. "How do you mean that word you are so fond of using today? I feel a little bit

148

confused by it, put off. . . . Do you mean repentance in the religious sense?"

"I just mean in the sense in which everyone uses the word!" Doris said sharply. "I don't know whether it's religious or not, but it's a perfectly good word and you know what it means. I want to have him show remorse."

"By the way, you aren't becoming religious, are you?" Joseph repeated. "It's so fashionable nowadays you might take it into your head to jump on the band wagon." He shook his finger playfully at her.

"God, no!" Doris answered fervently. "Still your idea may not be in his best interests after all. I imagine the people on the jury *are* religious, even if I am not! They will want to see some hint of a deeper emotion. . . . There are so many things to regret, even taking the girl to his room. That isn't very important as things worked out, but everything was so horrible and to have to add a little sordid detail like that is too much—"

"But he can't show what you're asking for without seeming to be guilty, you silly girl! And he certainly shows how sorry he is the girl is dead! And as for your little 'sordid detail' of the room, anyone would think you were a model of purity yourself—"

"I might have done the same thing, I don't deny it! I was fearless about breaking rules, but still I hope that if I died you would rather I didn't die in a men's rooming house even though you are not at all morally opposed to girls going to men's rooming houses!"

"This is too much for me," Parks muttered.

Doris was relieved to discontinue the conversation about the trial. It was clear that she could not explain what she

149

felt, that her emotions were of a nature she did not even wish to communicate to her husband. That most miserable of men—Rudy Peck. Heaven lost in the batting of an eye! In these last months all the sins of the world hung about him like an eternal dampness. His soul was the surface of the earth on a map, the wastes, oceans, mountains, and cities shrunken and flat, because there was nothing in his history except this great thing, this plane of horror, without shape or texture, an eternal moment. His face, his voice, his pleasant commonplaceness—all these affected Doris painfully. He was blinding, she could not like him, he was not to be endured in the flesh but only in some form of the imagination, as an actor, a symbol, going through a terrible fate, representing without actually being. What she couldn't bear was the awesome familiarity of Rudy Peck, the way in which he might have been anyone. And Betty Jane Henderson, together they were historic, our native couple, as sturdy and indigenous as our trees. When people of this typicality got out of control, it was as though nature herself screamed with pain. Something great was demanded to pay for it, to be able to return to the earth's ways.

Whenever Doris thought of the trial, a shabby, revolting evening in her own life invariably returned to her. While still in college she had spent a week end in New York with a friend. Hypnotically, the memory of herself on this evening came back to her. There she was again and again, glowing and giggling in a round-necked, black "cocktail" dress with a ribbon bow at the back of the waist, and her friend Louise in a black velvet skirt and blue satin blouse. They had five Martinis and no food. At

ten o'clock they had somehow been separated from their
friends and were, by a locomotion and intention impossible to grasp the next morning, in a taxi with two men
Doris and Louise despised, two strangers whom they were
treating with a drunken condescension which amounted to
coquettishness. Neither of the men was particularly young
and both of them worked in radio.

Doris's side of the taxi contained a news announcer
born in Michigan, a tight-lipped, nervous, pink-eyed man
with a large, fleshly nose, and a brutal indifference to
criticism. He thought himself famous, a personage, and
imagined he was an object of striking importance to these
absurd and very handsome college girls. "You're beautiful,
beautiful," the announcer hissed in her ear, his professionalism lending a dramatic cadence to the words. A hole
from a cigarette ash burned away in Doris's dress as she
gazed haughtily and with uncertainty upon her companion's greedy countenance.

Louise's sudden friend was a radio writer who lived in
an apartment on Riverside Drive, a tall, heavy man with a
small-mouthed grin, bleakly and shrewdly sentimental—
a sooty, smelly, and dusty person who roamed midtown
New York all day and half of the night and was as tired
as a postman. The taxi, stopping at dark bar after dark
bar; half-eaten sandwiches, coffee spilling into saucers:
even after five years all of this remained in Doris's memory. Fortunately she had felt sick that night and was de-
posited like a soiled handkerchief in the lobby of the hotel
where the two girls were staying, dropped off at two in the
morning. But Louise did not return until eight the next
day, and then with the pains of hell on her face she lay

silent and horrified the whole day long in the darkened room. She would not even look at Doris and they were never friendly again. The radio men had gone forever and yet they remained, a bruise of humiliation that shrank but did not vanish. Whenever Louise and Doris met afterward Louise's face turned quite pale with dislike for her friend. "These things happen," Doris bravely reassured herself, trying to cast off the galling remembrance of the sharp teeth of the radio announcer, the lump on her lip the next morning, the brown ash burn on her skirt. "How strange girls are," she concluded.

After a week or so of the melancholy idleness, Doris saw that there were not many possibilities in her present life and decided she might at least get a job. One morning with rare secretiveness and portentousness she left the house early, bent upon this errand. "Do you type?" they asked her at the University employment agency.

"Well, yes, a little, but not really professionally you know. I go pretty fast, but I make a lot of mistakes. When I want to do it perfectly, then I find it goes pretty slowly," she answered, twisting her pearls on her finger and with her head tilted to one side looking with pleasant and frank interest at the woman who questioned her. No, no, she didn't know a bit of shorthand. It was disappointing to learn that most of the interesting work at the University was already being done by someone else.

At last, still jauntily because she could not help but think of dull work as a gift she was capriciously offering, at last she said, shrinking only the least bit, she might work in the sociology library five hours a day, five days a week for eighty cents an hour. What a small amount of money that came to at the end of the week, not much at all, was her first discovery.

Leaving the appointment office, she stepped out in the glistening coldness, onto the paths crowded with students who were walking cautiously over the icy ground, beneath the gleaming shadows of conifers and the frozen, stripped branches of leaning maples. Doris liked cold weather. She wore red boots, a yellow scarf, fur mittens, and a heavy coat of checked tweed. All of this costume of costly woolens had been bought on her charge account at Best's. Several young men turned to look at her. On her way to the library she began to think of all the books she wanted to read at home, the important, fascinating things she might be doing. Now that she proposed to spend most of her day at a job, she longed to relearn her French, to have the time to begin on the list of philosophy books she had been carrying in her purse for the past year.

She was accepted at the library. Her superior was a young man—or was he young?—with a thin, brown mustache, horn-rimmed glasses, large rather dull eyes, and an appealing, indifferent smile. This was Mr. Emersen. "With an *e*," he said.

Doris was trying to write a glossy account of this new situation to her parents. Mr. Emersen was dispatched to them as "quite intelligent, I hope. Working his way through law school, he says."

The shutters of their garret apartment rattled noisily and Parks, pushed next to the window with the lamp almost resting on his shoulder, could see the waving tops of the trees. Fitfully he tried to read, even though from time to time he looked up surreptitiously at Doris, who sat frowning at her desk. Parks had the idea his wife wished to rebuke him for something. These ponderings and pencil chewings, her mysterious airs were puzzling. He dreaded a dangerous silence and did not know what to say when Doris came home in the evenings, the groceries under her arm, a somber and elegant expression on her face like that of a primitive saint. Her disarming sweetness when she washed the potatoes for baking, that gentle moan, the martyr's cry flying to heaven, when she found the broiler thick with last night's forgotten drippings which today defeated her dream of an effortless dinner. The light fell on Doris's strong and clumsy hands and Parks, seeing the curve of her breast, the dip of her blue jersey skirt and the wide red leather belt with gold bangles clanging on it was newly astonished by this girl who was his wife. What an ugly room this is, he thought, and Doris—what a beauty! Her very beauty was a reprimand.

"I'm not quite satisfied with myself," Doris said abruptly, giving her husband a mournful glance. "I mean even less than usual. . . . Waste, boredom, laziness . . ."

"My pretty old girl," Parks mumbled, reassuring himself. "I'm satisfied with you, perfectly!"

"You certainly took that standing up!" Doris said with energy. "I think it's very important to be at least reasonably satisfied with the life you're leading. And to feel the opposite, to feel it definitely and consciously, is quite demoralizing, take it from me!"

"What is it, dumpling?" Joe asked lightly.

"Well, to get down to brass tacks . . . it's all quite simple now that I think of it, quite simple really. The trouble is that I'm not doing anything worthwhile. I'm

154

ashamed of myself. I think the life I lead is disgusting. . . .
Well, that's a little strong, but at least it is stupid. I feel
stupid myself too, as if I had iron ore in my head."

"Your powers of speech are not paralyzed," Parks ventured with a laugh. "I'll feel more worried when that happens."

"Ah, that's where you're wrong! I am paralyzed in a
way. That's what I mean when I say my head feels heavy,
with iron ore in it," Doris continued in an insistent manner. "I guess I'm discovering what they call *old truths.*"

"And what are those, pray? I feel a little frightened by
the term somehow . . . especially when used by one so
young."

"Don't try to be funny, please. It's ghastly, but have you
noticed how people begin to resemble their parents as
soon as they get married? Someone who has seemed in
complete rebellion . . . all you have to do is get them
settled down and the woman begins to act just like her
mother and the man . . . he wants his meals served just
as father wanted them, wants his house run the same way.
. . . Now, recently I've been thinking lots of new things
. . . new for me at least. As I see it now, you've either got
to work, having an absorbing career, not just a job, or
else . . . don't yell, monster . . . or else a woman should
have children. Otherwise what relation has she got to anything? It seems to me she's not worth taking up space. You
get awfully dry without one or the other."

"Children!" Parks groaned. "I hate children! Just to
think of them makes me dizzy!"

"That's too bad about you—"

"A child would hate both of us, I promise you. I can

feel it resenting us and with good reason. . . . We'd probably be very unintelligent with it, just as other people are. . . . The way of all flesh, remember . . ."

"What way is that, clown?"

"Just what it says."

"I'm glad you didn't bring up that old saw about overpopulation and cannon fodder. If everyone thought that there wouldn't be a new generation. . . ."

"Your mathematics is right, but there is something to the argument, nevertheless. I would have brought it up next, if you had waited a moment."

"In this connection," Doris said thoughtfully, "your great trouble would be offensive doting."

"Tell it to your mother," Parks answered, smiling nervously.

In truth he was eaten up with curiosity about Doris's work at the library, but had not the courage to question her closely for fear of hearing something lacerating to his own feelings. The whole thing was a poison arrow piercing into his tender belief that he, at twenty-eight, was still a bud, an unopened green shoot too young to blossom. Parks had no doubt Doris was cherishing some operatic protest in her bosom; in her silences he heard screams of accusation; her docility was as sharp as a knife. The dullness of her work was threatening to his self-esteem—the whole thing seemed to have no purpose beyond his discomfort, a fact proved by the modesty of the earnings. Neither Parks nor Doris admitted the earning of small sums as a way of increasing one's income.

Doris added a few lines to her letter and, sighing, abandoned it again. About her husband she had written: "He's

156

still as strong as an ox, and he's often at his typewriter but won't show me what he's doing. I take that as a good sign of progress—you know, wanting things to be perfect before anyone sees them."

She sat back dreamily, thinking of her mother's life, computing like an accountant at his ledger, adding and subtracting to her mother's score by the measure of her own life.

It was not an easy operation: the very existence of Doris herself, her mother's child, was a sum she did not know how to reckon with. For the rest there was a good share of the housework and cooking, the marketing, gardening, charitable afternoons at the Episcopal Church, one morning a month "donated" to the public health center. Most of all there was grandmother, that ancient, imperishable, numb doll of ninety years who breathed half-heartedly but interminably on the third floor. Doris's mother nursed and coddled this creature loyally, with all the passion of a scruple and sometimes with madness nearly. The echo of their conversations made Doris shiver. "Mother! Mother! Cousin Susie's in Florida . . . Florida . . . Cousin Susie!" Grandmother was deaf, and the conversations were an offering, piercing screams of sentiment, a heart-rending pantomime, flowers for the dead. Doris examined these matters and reached her usual conclusion, which was a bit of dialogue with herself, "Of course, children are inclined to think their parents accept everything, but still I don't think Mother questions her life as much as I do. That's just a fact, neither good nor bad."

Idly, tauntingly, Doris continued her previous line with

Joseph, "Pet, if we had children how would you support them?" She turned a clear and cruel eye upon him.

"I don't see how I could just now," Parks said with dignity. "I don't quite see it at the moment."

"I didn't say just at this moment, this very minute. What about later or ever! It's quite an undertaking. I marvel at the courage other men reveal! . . . Some of the people here working on Ph.D's have more than one child, all of them living in trailers and Quonset huts. Baby and all, everything in its place, little bunk beds, laundry racks . . ."

"If we had children I'd have to support them—or *it!* It's just one of those things one must do when the occasion arrives. I'd set about finding a way and find it, as everyone else does. . . . That's that when these things happen. . . . There's nothing so mysterious about it. . . ."

"What would you do, what sort of work?" Doris put in without a pause.

"I can't imagine at the moment, naturally," Parks replied in a hollow voice. Hesitating, he recovered his strength. "A child doesn't necessarily profit by having everything easy. It needn't be spoiled or expect advantages beyond the ordinary. . . . Indeed, I feel very strongly about these things and even if it were possible I wouldn't like to raise a child selfishly. . . ."

"But even the ordinary things you are talking about cost quite a bit, believe me! I think it is hard going for the least, for the necessities. And a good education, really good, is something else again."

"The public, free schools *are* education in this country,

fortunately, and the state universities. I should think that would be the very least of our worries."

"Yes, I suppose so. Maybe so," Doris said darkly.

She supported her chin with her hand and it seemed to Parks that her glance was malicious. He remembered their courtship, picnics, swimming pools, driving into New York to hear Dixieland jazz bands. He remembered also the rival he had defeated so easily because the other boy was, as Doris expressed it, "worthlessly attractive and much too successful!"—an opinion fully justified by the fact that the young man was even then earning several hundred dollars a week in an advertising agency.

"Some of the trees' branches are cracking," Parks said in an inspired tone, delighted for this diversion. "The wind is very strong. . . . Would you think I was crazy if I went out in it?"

"No, not at all. I love storms," Doris agreed. "If I weren't going to wash my hair I'd go out with you."

Outside on the dark streets Parks felt his spirits revived. He walked rapidly, even though he had to step carefully to avoid falling branches. It made him feel glorious to be on foot this way, since of course he and Doris had an automobile, a not very old Plymouth sedan which had formerly belonged to Parks's mother. They dearly wished to sell this car and with some extra money which would surely come from somewhere buy a Morris sports car. "I hate these fat American cars," Doris often said. "You'd feel positively elegant in one of the cheaper, more sensible foreign ones."

Through the residential section, Parks made his way to the shopping center where he found the fire department busy with ladders, propping up a great beer sign on the roof of a drugstore. Parks loved crowds, and *downtown*, anywhere, Main Streets and Broadways. He liked shop windows, magazine stands, street corners, and taverns. To hear strains of music as he passed a house or a bar filled him with the joy of life. Sensations of this nature, his pounding heart as he eavesdropped on other people's conversation, had given him the idea that he should be a writer. A heart and mind so easily swept away by the common things of life must be an indication of something special. His joy and curiosity were endowments as queer and determining as the gift for mathematics or perfect pitch.

He entered a bright tavern with a loud jukebox and ordered a glass of beer at the bar. How young all these people are! he thought, observing the college couples with a kindly, rather sorrowful eye. Yes, these students were about twenty years old and Parks was nearly a decade older, but they were the same age in the most important sense. All of them had grown up in a period of devastating war, political chaos, and matchless prosperity. It occurred to Parks that these Iowa students did not look any different from those of his expensive prep-school memories or from his Dartmouth days. He could not even see their "newness," which he knew to exist, for they were the children of farmers who in ten years had stepped from the pickup truck in which the family went visiting on a Sunday to a Buick for themselves and often these proud, grinning, weather-red citizens could not refuse a second car for their boy or girl in college.

No doubt the farm parents still did a great deal of extremely hard work, and perhaps their furniture, beloved, unsoiled objects, was sometimes a bit "tacky" in its heavy, opulent design, but their daughters were debutantes, smiling, knowing, brilliantly, richly simple in their *Mademoiselle* college clothes, their short haircuts and great expectations. Amazing histories! Parks liked to think, imagining himself explaining it all to some friend in the East. Yes, yes, nodding philosophically, they drive Cadillacs and have been known to spend a part of the winter in Florida. But why not? How petty was the resentment of

161

those who scorned this advance, that *ancien régime* whose only requirement was that one had grown no richer in the last fifteen years, that aristocracy which looked down on the new house, the improved kitchen!

Parks did not share this resentment, certainly not, but still he could not quite admit the wealth which climbed up to the simple, plain cottage door like a wild, democratic vine. By wealth Parks, with his old-fashioned nature, meant city mansions, gruff old men who drove to the Stock Exchange in black limousines. Parks had some of the bantam belligerence, the boozy exhilaration of Irishmen long after the revolution who remembered the old troubles with a tear and missed the old cruelties. He could sometimes regret that the labor unions were so successful they did not need the services of bright, enthusiastic, charitable persons like himself. Communists, Trotskyites, conservative ex-Communists, pacifists—how he envied them all, this man of a later day. His times were out of joint—poor Parks growing up in environments in which it was difficult even to find someone to give old clothes to. There was almost a gratifying sorrow in Rudy Peck's father, a man left behind by history, a figure to inspire a young man of generous impulses.

At the bar in the pink glare Parks struck up a conversation with a quiet, thin-faced boy sitting next to him. From the very beginning, Parks noticed his solitary neighbor, a young man neatly dressed in white shirt, figured tie, sharply pressed blue suit. But on his hands there were grease marks which all the fastidiousness in the world could not entirely wash away. This was Thomas Drew, Rudy Peck's old friend, who was waiting, he said, for the wind to die down so that he could drive home some twenty miles away.

"It's a tricky storm," Parks agreed.

Over the din of the bar they could make out a few phrases in a news broadcast which went over the events that day at Rudy's trial. "It's a great tragedy," Parks said. "He seems to be a pretty decent sort of fellow."

He noticed that the young man bit his lip and wondered what this might mean. "Are they much interested in the trial over your way? What are they saying about it? I'm just a student here and so I don't really know the state as a whole."

"What are they saying? I wouldn't quite know how to size that up," Drew replied and so softly Parks could hardly hear him.

Parks was heartened by this, even though Drew certainly did not indicate any desire to converse and kept looking nervously toward the door, judging the wind. Still Parks could feel some response to Rudy's trial although he could not judge its nature.

"As I said, I don't know anyone from other towns. Here there is quite a bit of sympathy for the boy and some worry that he won't get a square deal. Yes, I'd say a lot of people are sympathetic—"

"Are they? I'm glad to hear that," Drew said, blushing and turning away from Parks.

"I take that to mean you're sympathetic too," Parks said, draining his glass and offering another round to Drew, who declined. This was more than Parks had hoped for, this chance to talk with a native who shared some of his emotion about the prisoner. "It's a sort of Dreiser thing," he

163

added in his evangelistic tone. But immediately Parks regretted this move because he saw his companion did not understand him. "I mean he is a poor boy, wanting the bright things of life . . . a pretty girl, one who had had things easier . . . difficulty with her parents . . ."

"Oh, it was that you think?" Drew said quickly, turning his worn, intense face to Parks.

"It seems so to me as I look at it. Of course, it is not easy to get the whole thing pieced together, but that is a part of it . . . the—what shall I call it?—the class or social difference between the two people."

Before his eyes, Parks suddenly had the sensation of great slum scenes, one after another, flowing on forever. He remembered the outskirts of Chicago—the massiveness of those flimsy, tall wooden tenements, black, peeled, leaning towers of filth, damp, dirt, and rusting tin. Back porches, dingy yards under a cloud of train and factory soot, strewn with ruins and relics of ancient times, old tires, car parts, wash tubs, potsherds from the five and ten.

"Yes," Parks expanded. "This boy, Peck, appears to be collegiate, or whatever you want to call it. . . . He is that, since it's not a crime! But his real character goes deeper, I believe. He's put together in layers, I sometimes think. . . . People who go up the ladder tend to be like that. . . . You see, his father was a factory worker and not even a native American, I believe, although I'm not quite sure. As a family they were fine people but they hadn't an easy time of it, at least not always. And I think even the son must have some sense of not quite belonging. Something of that came into his relationship with the girl. She was pretty, charming, and popular and it is understandable

164

that he would have cared for her, but you feel it was more than that, that she had a value to him all out of proportion, an imaginary quality . . ."

Drew's eyes did not leave Parks's face. What a quiet, strange person he is, Parks thought, slightly disarmed and hesitating to continue, wondering if perhaps the young man were not the son of factory workers himself. "Do you see what I mean?" he inquired with a smile.

"No," Drew answered, blinking.

"You think Peck is just a criminal, without any special complications?"

Drew started, still looking with wonder at Parks. "No, no, not that at all!" He paused, staring and blinking stupidly. "Certainly not what you say. He's . . . I don't know. . . . It was different, not quite as you have it . . . his life, not bad . . . not bad at all . . ."

"What? What was not *bad?*" Parks asked, heavily underscoring the word and yet trying to establish some sort of camaraderie with the skinny, foolishly staring boy beside him.

"His life . . . I mean . . ."

"Oh, I never meant to suggest anything morally bad or lacking. . . . How funny that you should take it that way. . . . I meant insecure, uneasy, not certain where he belonged—"

"Oh!" Drew said, now without any expression at all, but shyly, secretly there, searching the astounded Parks. "Oh, yes, I see. . . ."

He looked at his watch and then softly said to Parks, smiling and smiling, "I must go. Even if I get blown off the highway. . . . My wife is waiting. . . . I drove over

165

here after dinner . . . on business for my father and expected to be back an hour ago—"

He stood for a moment, buttoning slowly his fancy overcoat with wide, padded shoulders and large buttons in the shape of acorns. Suddenly a look of pain and hesitation curtained his face; his jaws twitched as if he had a toothache. He started to speak, "I—" and then turning and lowering his head he at last only said, "So long," and went away.

At the door, Thomas Drew turned back to look at Parks and then suddenly was gone.

Parks felt somewhat depressed by this encounter and even when he had forgotten all about Drew the depression lingered on fitfully, seeping into his deepest being and flooding him with questions. He regretted that he could not at will summon up great dreams of himself as a writer. "We've come upon the world at a difficult moment," he decided. For himself, at least, he wanted very little, believed very little to be possible. It was a comforting guarantee to know there was nothing outrageous in his dreams. Their very modesty recommended them to him.

The depression lifted and with a purposeful step he went to the telephone booth to look up Professor Mitchell's address. He discovered that Anita lived on a street which he might have passed on his way home at any time. That he seldom ever chose this way merely surprised him. Tonight he was following the wind—the fierceness of the blow made every step dramatic. I like this town, really like it, Parks admitted suddenly, happy to be able to offer his approval.

Entire living rooms with the window blinds lifted to the

top in the way of small towns were to be seen glowing through the swaying, crackling trees. The street lights were swinging like old lanterns, in the cozy, warm houses children were studying around the dining-room table—what a gleam of life and naturalness there was in all this. "Here is where I belong at this period in my life," Parks said grandly. "True it is not immediately profitable, but on the other hand it isn't as if I were doing anything harmful."

He found Anita Mitchell's house easily. There it was, circled round with a now useless front porch upon which families no longer sat summer and winter because of the street crowded with cars. Still one could imagine the original owners on the porch during a hot afternoon, all of them fanning, drinking iced tea. Inside, the house still called for large family Sunday dinners at the heavy mahogany dining table with the mother passing plates loaded with meat, vegetables, and last of all a tremendous angel food cake.

Anita's long spotless windows with severe draperies and queer, stringy plants like abstract drawings gave Parks a rush of timidity. The scene was not hospitable—it asked one to live up to it, he thought, as he stood across the street looking. And then he saw Anita herself. Her frail, long-necked image passed the window as though she were on a stage set. What an unusual and lonely woman, Parks thought indulgently, now crossing the street rapidly, his actions irrationally, romantically justified by the velocity and wildness of the wind. A blown and friendly messenger out of the night, he saw himself enthusiastically.

Anita answered his knock immediately, appearing very

167

quickly before him in a Chinese mandarin coat of black satin. "Oh, it's you!" she said smoothly, asking him to come in as if he were a usual caller.

"No, I can't stay," Parks said gaily. "This is a strange coincidence and I couldn't resist knocking! I was just walking along and by some chance saw you through your window. I wanted to warn you. . . . The wind seems to be coming faster and faster. Downtown there's quite a bit of broken glass, shattered windows, that sort of thing. . . . A huge sign over the drugstore nearly came loose and fell to the street, but they got it before it actually crashed. . . ."

"I still have my senses intact," Anita said, laughing. "I am aware of the wind, but I'm glad you came to rescue me." Parks stepped inside the doorway.

He was enchanted with Anita and with himself. How he liked her! How many good things he wished her! Just then she shivered and, going close to her, Parks touched her arm tenderly. Anita looked up at him and then with a tragic expression, both self-deprecating and amazed, her face collapsed and her thin, taut features crumpled into tears. "I'm so sorry. . . . I'm terribly tired. . . . Ridiculous of me, but I am so tired. . . ."

Parks, stunned by the scene, kissed her cold forehead and followed her into the living room. Immediately Anita was under control again. "God, how extraordinary that was!" she exclaimed, wiping her eyes. "Isn't it fantastic! I've never done anything so stupid."

"No, no," Parks said sweetly. "It was nothing to be alarmed about!"

"I must seem a perfect fool," Anita said, now smiling. "I think it was the cold wind stinging my eyes. Coming out

168

into it so suddenly, perhaps. I must watch that in the future. . . . These tragic outbursts mustn't become a habit!"

The tears had made them both feel remarkably comfortable, *en famille* as it were, like a temper tantrum. Parks looked around the charming room, admiring its ascetic perfection even though for his own part he liked things lumpier, fatter, warmer.

Anita made hardly a sound in her slippers of golden thread when she went for the brandy glasses, little green thimbles edged with silver.

"What pretty glasses!" Parks said, inanely happy.

"They aren't *really* good," Anita said with a shrug. "Nothing at all special . . . I got them here at an auction sale."

"Everything is very nice, very interesting," Parks insisted with a round gesture which took in the whole living room. On the mantel ivy trailed up the two sides of a mirror.

"Do you like it? Sometimes I think it's dreary," Anita said warmly. "I *am* fastidious, I am! It can't be helped, I suppose, a disease some people have. But I do realize how boring it is. I work and clean and polish just like all the other women . . . and it's worse to want to make things a little different, to have these vulgar aspirations! You know . . . cobbler's benches for cocktail tables, or drop-leaf affairs from the junk store, and my rocker with the needlepoint seat . . . There must be two dozen just like it within ten blocks. . . ." Parks tried to express his disagreement with this low estimate by raising his hands in mock horror, but Anita proceeded, a certain huskiness in

169

her voice which Parks had not detected before. "Do you suppose rich people's houses look any different from the usual run of middle-class establishments? . . . I mean really rich people! . . . I doubt it. If they have things *too* grand, marble, and immense, valuable objects, silver bathroom fittings . . . then it's just bad taste, cold and ostentatious. . . . People would laugh! But the trouble is that if things are not prohibitively expensive then everyone has them, every little housewife who reads the ladies magazines and fancies herself a decorator. . . . It's very hard to win!"

"Does it matter?" Parks said in friendly reproach.

"Yes, it does in a way. . . . I'm an incurable snob!" Anita tossed her head merrily as she said this.

"No, just saying it proves you aren't!"

"What nonsense! Not in the least! I'd give my soul to be really distinguished looking and to live in a quiet, rich, elegant way, quite different from most people's . . . but so subtly it wouldn't be recognized except by people who lived in the same way. . . . And I would love to have a slave, an old-fashioned *body servant*. . . . Not just to do the work, because I'm first-rate at that myself. No, I'd love someone bobbing in and out, wearing a black and white costume, turning down beds at night, and answering the door even when you're sitting there with nothing else to do yourself. . . . Are you shocked, you great leveler?"

"Well, no," Parks replied loftily. "I don't take all this seriously."

"No, it isn't serious in a certain sense but only in that it isn't a possibility. But it shows you what kind of trivial daydreams I have in my head sometimes. . . . That's the way you get to know people's weak spots."

Parks remarked after a pause, "You're rather hard on yourself tonight, Mrs. Mitchell."

"I'm only admitting to those faults I'm secretly proud of," Anita answered slyly. "Don't you think we all do that? . . . And nothing more. . . . We're very skillful in concealing our true nightmares and unflattering desires."

"I suppose we are or try to be," Parks conceded, although he could not imagine any such dreadful secrets as he enjoyed Anita's quite agreeable appearance, her smooth hair and thick, perfectly arched eyebrows. She was a "creation," a work of portraiture, especially in the stillness and composure of her features. And it took a bit of nerve to seek such an effect, that he knew, wondering where it came from, how out of her queer shyness she had shaped this extraordinarily noticeable style and smartness.

Anita explained that her husband was not at home this evening. He had gone to a college fifty miles away for a lecture, and had telephoned he would spend the night there because of the storm. "I'm awfully glad he didn't try to come back. It's much too dangerous, but then he hates staying away from home, especially visiting people . . . and so it's miserable for the poor fellow either way."

Anita said this without a trace of flirtatiousness. It was followed by a pause in the conversation which revealed how little they had to say to each other that did not somehow include their passionate interest in the destiny of Rudy Peck.

"I have a friend who is making a study of the way the press is handling the case, a statistical and attitude study

171

combined. He seems to think there has been a growing hostility to Rudy in the papers in the last couple of days." Parks felt grateful for this studious friend.

"I feel more hopeless every day about it," Anita said vibrantly. "These things can hardly be expected to turn out anyway except more or less disastrously, I suppose. . . . Actually, it should be decided in privacy, in a doctor's office, and not in a law court. In the end the people who must decide are asked to do more than they can rightly do. They haven't any notion of modern psychology, through no fault of their own, of course. They couldn't be expected to. But think of it! It's as though you had a bunch of alchemists on a poison case!"

"It's very disheartening, yes," Parks said mournfully.

Anita went on breathlessly. "I don't know whom to fear the most. The men or the women on the jury. Men are often inclined to harshness, especially when they have the backing of morality and convention, because they need in this way to restrain their own aggressive instincts, to deny them by censuring the same thing in another!"

"You fill me with gloom," Parks said.

"The men would be afraid of overidentifying with Rudy. It's not just a matter of sympathizing with the girl as of the fear perhaps of their own deep-seated lack of sympathy, their own destructive instincts toward women from the mother down to their wives and daughters. . . . That is what will lead them to be severe, I think. . . ."

"You make me afraid of my fellow creatures!" Parks interrupted, attempting to lighten the conversation which was not going in the way he found most cheerful.

"All unconsciously, I mean. They will have to punish

172

this boy as they punish their own thoughts. They must be hostile to him because they reject a certain side of themselves—the side that doesn't feel the tenderness and protectiveness for women they are supposed to feel. Quite the contrary, many men see women as a threat to their very being, as a force trying to destroy them . . . and there is a deep psychological truth in that sometimes. . . ."

"Truth?" Parks said lamely.

"A kind of truth," Anita answered with a bold glance at him. "There is a threat from the mother, even after the mother is dead. Representing the attraction of childhood, irresponsibility, passivity. What Jung, I think it was, called the *terrible mother!* She bears all the guilt and blame, the secret guilt. A man is his own master and yet he never ceases to be afraid of the nightmare image pulling him back, engulfing him, emasculating him."

"Yes, Jung is very interesting, I believe. I've not read him as carefully and thoroughly as you have," Parks said, accepting a second thimbleful of brandy.

"And the women serving on the jury. Sometimes I resent them! It's outrageous, ridiculous, I know it. And yet sometimes they seem *so* foolish to me and I can't help my feelings. I'm sure they are good sorts in fact, mindful of their civic and maternal duties . . . too much so! Such profound seriousness and earnestness! Their startled eyes . . . their hands crossed in their laps . . . But I'm not sure I trust that kind of seriousness. Is it enough? Often it seems to be just a form of self-congratulation!"

Parks smoked and listened. "What do you think their attitude is? The women's?"

"Of course, one can't say, but how could it, speaking

realistically, possibly be deep enough for a thing of this kind? You know how women are, proud of their horror, their frayed nerves, their cringings and gaspings over everything . . . tears. . . . But they don't like in the end to face up to the complexity of things, the difficult relations between men and women as groups, between themselves and their children. . . . Mothers are absolutely bowled over, I'm sure—even the youngest and most advanced ones —bowled over by what the simplest work of psychology has to say about the Oedipus complex, infantile behavior, or childhood. . . ." Here Anita stopped, brushed the arm of the sofa, and gathering breath finally said very softly, "Sexuality, childhood sexuality, as it is called." That hurdle passed, she swept on, "Those who profess to be serious about such things secretly reveal that they think it's a lot of nonsense, at least in the case of their own children! Haven't they had babies! Haven't they nursed and studied them day and night without running into any of these complexes! A baby is a baby, a child is a child! Those little things aren't something out of Greek drama!"

"So you think the women are against him?" Parks interrupted, feeling uneasy. He and all his friends discussed "psychology" and he believed it without having any devouring interest in this line of inquiry. Yet it was clear beyond a doubt that the jury could not be asked to undergo the self-purification and self-analysis Anita considered a prelude to justice. "You're quite a specialist in this sort of thing," he said dimly, "criminal psychology. . . ."

"Criminal psychology!" Anita repeated angrily. "He's not a *criminal*, if anyone is in the old sense! That's just the point. . . . And I'm not a specialist in anything."

"No, he's certainly not a criminal! You've mistaken my meaning, my intention—"

"My idea is that he got into a deep psychological tangle. . . . It is very deep indeed and yet very common at the same time. There's no love affair, no marriage that hasn't a touch of the same thing in it. This case is very nearly a prototype of all the anxieties, destructive wishes, frustrations! The dream of killing the person you love . . . it's as old as the human race. . . . What is it all about? That's the question. . . ."

"Do you think he's guilty?" Parks asked in a conspiratorial whisper.

"I couldn't possibly judge," Anita replied. "I'm not God. . . . I don't know. But if it did happen in that way, *even if it did,* even then, you've got to grasp the psychological meaning. One thing is certain . . . he's not depraved, not dangerous, not driven to kill people. This is a particular tragedy and probably it shows what a need there is for psychiatrists and a need for public education, so that people will seek the services of such psychiatrists as are available."

"No doubt," Parks said without much expression. "Or if he had had more of his rightful share of the worldly goods, especially as a youngster when the character is forming. We're certainly more democratic than most countries, but in the long run we have our own rigid class system nearly as complete as the Hindus. . . . Our untouchables . . . Rudy's poverty in his youth, his foreign parents . . . that can make an enormous difference. The girl was in the deepest sense ordinary enough and her situation was not an unusually privileged one. . . . But if

175

you look at it in the terms of the local drama and every-
day desires so important to people she was something quite
special to him. Her parents' objection to the match must
have outraged Peck's finest feelings, made him doubt his
own value—"

"I don't think the girl paid any attention to her parents!"

"Even if she grew tired of him in the most natural way,
he may have *thought* it had something to do with social
inferiority. . . . We can't, as a society, instill that sort of
fear and shame in people without expecting it to have
consequences, disastrous ones. . . ."

Anita was looking at her fingernails. "His life is ruined,"
she said in a forlorn voice, "and for what?"

Anita's thinness charmed and grieved Parks. "Are you
cold?" he asked.

"No, certainly not!"

"You know you mustn't worry too much about all
this—" .

"I'm not in any danger. . . . One's sense of justice—"

"Yes, the sense of justice."

"It will all be over soon and we'll forget soon enough!
I wonder what happens to such people. There must be
quite a few of them in the world, people who have had
extraordinary sufferings, been tested by fire. It is not too
hard to endure sorrow when all the world sorrows with
you, but to have to take it alone, with humiliation and
the world's distrust thrown in . . . that is not fair! For
myself I think I would rather die."

Parks had no thought of falling in love with Anita. He
and all his friends were exceptionally faithful husbands.

176

And yet, being here with this strange and diverting woman called to mind other girls he had cared for. Devotion was Parks's striking quality as a lover. He was always a bit slow to know what women were thinking and in the past had been frequently surprised to learn that a love affair had begun or ended, both of these events taking place while his back was turned, so to speak. He held in the greatest esteem all the girls who had once been fond of him, and he had, before his serious pursuit of Doris, been somewhat courageously "engaged" three times.

Parks's most memorable experience had been a girl who studied dancing at Bennington College: Norina, short and knotty, with a twist of brown hair on the top of her head like a country woman. She liked nothing better than loosening this twist, letting her hair fall down to her shoulders in preparation for a dance demonstration—this sudden fall of hair providing scenery, costume, and mystery for her performance. Norina saw a great deal of Parks for four or five months before he went into the army and sometimes he stayed overnight in her studio, a loft near the clotted, dark docks of the Hudson River. He could still remember with a pain her studio room, sparsely furnished with square tables of plywood which rested on cement blocks; and those dark green wine bottles filled with rhododendron branches that cast shadows on the wall, giving the place a tropical austerity like a bittersweet hideaway in a Conrad tale.

Norina had the ability to become a charming memory in only a few seconds. One night she told Parks she didn't believe she wanted to see him again, and she spoke this verdict with such friendliness, unconcern, and mysterious

177

decision that Parks was obliged to accept it in the same spirit. Yet he had never altogether ceased to puzzle in odd moments about the dizzy swiftness of the conclusion, the "what had happened." Remaining with him were the kindliest regards for his image of Norina's little pug-dog face, her leaps and enthralling barefoot choreography.

He rose to leave. "Yes, it is rather late," Anita agreed. "I do thank you for dropping by."

"Thank me! You are the one to be thanked," Parks said with tenderness. "I enjoyed it very much. . . . I hope you sleep well."

"I will, I will," Anita assured him hastily, not detaining him.

At the door they were met by Harold March. Parks remembered Anita's mention of this young man and looked at him with genuine and rather miserable interest. Irrationally he found himself feeling that March's very existence was a nuisance, March a perfect stranger to him. From the very first Parks decided he didn't like Mrs. Mitchell's roomer and this decision made him vaguely unhappy as they all said good night.

At home Parks found Doris fast asleep. Her hair was twisted into wet curls and a hairpin lay on her cheek, having escaped beneath her yellow satin headband. I wonder what she is dreaming about? Parks asked himself. Carefully he emptied the ash tray by the bed and placed Doris's reading glasses in a safe spot on the bookcase. Her damp curls reminded him of Anita's tears.

Anita and Parks became a familiar couple as the trial went into its last days. Seeing them standing about talking and smoking during the recess, one might have thought they were official observers from the keenness of their interest, the brilliance of their memories for each word said on the stands, and the earnest, debating, disputing manner in which they went over each step. They shared few ideas about the case, but this was not nearly so disabling as one would think since they at least shared a profound uncertainty about most of the other spectators, a desperate concern about the intellectual agility of the jury, a fascinated disapproval of the cold busyness of the reporters who did not seem to "care" how the trial turned out. This latter circumstance caused Parks, who had been previously much attracted to the newspaper profession, now to mark it off his list of future possibilities for himself. He gave the occupation an indifferent rating on the score of morality. Hardened by the constant state of crisis of which they were the historians, the reporters could honestly lay claim to objectivity. But the very fullness of their views shrank their sensibilities, corseted their personalities: or so Parks believed after his scrutiny of the press table. These men and women often misrepresented facts in their headlines, like a lusty barker describing a tame show within, but the actual news stories in their completeness gave everything without emphasis. The reporters were in the end denied the drama of ennobling prejudice. Rudy, as he emerged daily from the presses of a dozen papers, was a mingled yarn, threatening sometimes in the dark print, excused in a paragraph.

It seemed to the two apprehensive partisans, Anita and Parks, hardly just that this trial would last only ten days. They felt it needed to be studied, considered, weighed in the manner of a commission delegated to come to a decision. Naturally, they knew this was a radical, unprecedented notion and so they could only vaguely state it to each other as a theme on a Utopian agenda. Not even ten full days, only ten short-houred days with comfortable intermissions. The intermissions acknowledged the fatigue of those called upon to decide a young man's future, a weariness of the flesh and the burdened mind. The subject streamed out into its intolerable complications. If the jurors showed mercy here, it meant indifference there. They had Rudy's life on the one hand and the young girl's death on the other, both lying before them, unholy puzzles. Somehow the grief of Betty Jane's parents had to be recognized, that grief which had spread over their lives like an exterminating poison, paralyzing their spirits. The jury was called upon to judge whether Rudy's parents would henceforth live in injured innocence, wondering if they could ever forgive the nightmare days of accusation— this if he were found innocent. Or if these two people were to be struck by lightning, split in two forever, sent downward into misery without hope. Worst of all they were called, eight Iowa men and four women, to protect society itself, themselves, their neighbors—they were soldiers on this strange battle front. To this load of contradictory demand was added the hope of satisfying the varied, intense opinion of those who followed the case—and respect for the abstract law itself. All this must be done and allow for dismissal before the shops and food markets were closed in the late afternoon.

Around the lobby one could hear the echoes of humble dogmatisms, the buzzing of tenets expected and outlandish, repetitions of obvious considerations and additions of soaring originality.

One old man, haunter of courtrooms and warm public libraries, of the race which hates privacy and loves a studious, speculative public life, this old man with a face of fair, Swedish equity, a lonely, aggressive, quick flow of talk, the rush of one who has been cut off in the middle of a thousand conversations, sounded his refrain: "They know more than they're telling! A lot of secret material is being withheld from the public! They know more than they're telling!" His *they* was an honest plural. Everyone, Rudy, his lawyers, the sheriff, the judge, the jurors, the doctors, the police, the very secretaries who loyally continued even while the trial progressed to give out forms for driving tests: all these the old man believed to be in the possession of odds and ends of fact and fancy which he would dearly like himself to be allowed to chew upon. There was, he thought, an inside story which his open, Scandinavian intelligence felt should be shared by all. "There's more, there's more," he insisted.

"She wasn't playing fair with him!" a stout lady in-

181

toned, honoring some phantasmagorical dream of a betraying siren, a wicked coquette, a calamitous charmer. "That type gets in trouble."

Anita and Parks grew used to these eccentrics who gave out their ideas to everyone like a calling card. But often they heard mumblings and grumblings of hostility to Rudy voiced by very intelligent and serious persons and these froze them in their tracks.

They overheard a lawyer from another town, a sallow but alert man whom many people seemed to know: "I'd say he deserves a pretty heavy sentence! It seems to me that we owe leniency in other places, where there hasn't been much chance or opportunity. I'd say this one had let everyone down. . . . If you give him a short sentence, that means for reclamation and all that. . . . But he's not a young, handicapped boy in need of reform. . . . He's bright, educated, had all the chance in the world. . . . Doesn't look much good to me."

"You're assuming guilt—" a friend objected.

"Yes, I am that!" the lawyer said.

Or sometimes they would hear someone say with a shrug, "It all comes down to a simple fact. You can't go around killing people!"

A dread and weightiness changed everything as the trial went on and came near the end. The frightfulness of it all, the death, the trial, the verdict covered the process with its chill. The town buses, rusty brown, groaned along their streets, trucks with heavy loads continued along Route 6. Rudy, straightening his tie, seemed to be saying, "I am one with you all, you Iowans . . . a busy man . . . and depressed by the long winters."

182

"Things will look better when the witnesses for the defense appear," Parks said. "Rudy's character witnesses will be next, I understand."

"And what will they mean by *character?*" Anita asked carelessly.

High-school teachers, ministers, and friends from Rudy's home town spoke on his behalf, testified to his acceptable scholarship, his sportsmanship and pleasant behavior at all times. These men, utterly reputable, even outstanding for high-mindedness, sober, responsible, spoke briefly, isolating Rudy's adolescent history from all the others around him, summing him up neatly, or trying to. "Never any trouble with him. Always dependable," or "moral reputation always good," and "perfect record, never even had a parking ticket so far as I know," and "sort of guy who never lost his temper."

Parks felt his emotions touched by these people. What a depth of calm gravity one sometimes saw in these men and women who had spent their lives with young people, one group after another coming along as regularly as the seasons. They seemed to carry in their minds the memory of ten thousand report cards, yearly ratings, and vague impressions of tardy marks long ago. Yes, there was a sort of trembling at the edge of their lips from decades of conferences, rebukes, and recommendations, facing up to embarrassing scenes, meeting the same old vices every autumn and dismissing the same careless lot every June. They were parents of an impossibly large family, their disappointments ludicrously multiplied, their failures spoiling bright morning after bright morning. How many clever, promising faces they had seen suddenly go sullen never to clear again, all without a heralding of any sort. The surprises these teachers and counselors had to endure were infinite, for the jerky minds under their care did not think of their comfort. How confusing it is for them after all, Parks thought with sympathy. The mediocre, the unlikely, the difficult, will turn and churn and shape themselves anew, bursting forth brilliantly all of a sudden, while the guardian's back was turned. It is always the unexpected with which these patient leaders have to deal and they have, thereby, an expression of cautiousness, sometimes dismay that these fruits and flowers follow no law—the trees inclining unmindful of the bend in the branches only a short time past. Their tears are for the abrupt, and their thoughtful eyes would look again at their own nature, undermined by these years of false predictions. Trancelike, these impressions came to Parks as he followed the questions and answers in the court.

"Tell me," a man on his right said suddenly, punching Parks in his ribs and awakening him from his dreaming, "do you always stand up when the judge comes in or just once a day?"

"Ah, each time, I think. I'm not sure," Parks replied, astonished.

"I just wondered. That's the custom in our town too, and I wondered how the judge liked to have it done here."

"Have you come from far?" Parks said.

"About seventy miles. Had a little time off today . . . our work is slow just now, building business . . . thought I'd take it in," the man whispered, seeing the judge look in their direction.

Parks would have liked to ask him more, but did not

wish to be reprimanded by the court and so he turned his attention back to the last of the character witnesses. Rudy, the "decent, honest, ordinary boy" the witnesses had been describing, strained nearer to these friends, crushing them fast to his heart.

There was a break for some discussion among the lawyers. At this point Parks meditatively ventured, "I'd say there's been a slight falling off since the high-school days, a shift in character here and there. A decline, perhaps, slight as I said before." It was painful for Parks to speculate about this. The past was a bit hard to find again, the recollections were of a time one could not exactly trust. The thickening, the coarsening, every year contributed to it, not only for Rudy but for everyone. Parks had had this sensation before when he looked at his parents' wedding photograph. He did not care to be reminded of that lost freshness, of the earliest bloom on the bush.

"I don't mean to suggest anything immoral coming now, later. You understand what I mean. The fraternities, the confusion at college, class grades not quite so good. I know the pressure gets greater, you change, want more out of life, make mistakes—"

"Not at all!" Anita said testily. "I don't think there's been any falling off, as you express it! I feel quite the opposite. Those little high-school prudes don't mean a thing, those boy scouts and class presidents. It's not promising to continue in that way, doesn't show enough imagination. Excellence is another thing altogether. I won't say he had that, but he had more of it in college than he did in his goody days. What did you want him to do? Be a grind, be nothing? When something goes wrong, doesn't work out

safely, all you people suddenly become in love with mediocrity. You start yelling that if he'd only been mediocre
everything would have been all right! For my part, I think
it's to his credit that he had enough imagination to push
forward, if only to that silly fraternity, to the girl. He
might have set his cap higher, but that would have been
asking too much!"

More medical men were brought to the scene. Apparently the state felt their evidence to be incontrovertible,
even though this evidence was often of the most high-
flown sort, as brilliant and suggestive as a poem. The continuing mystery of the human body—there is hardly a case
nowadays, the papers explained, in which the doctors do
not play their immense part. The dead must be amazed
to learn that trying to escape the path of a gun or surprised in attack the body's sad bone and muscle may turn
in such a way as to free the slayer.

Two of the doctors believed that Betty Jane had, at least
by implication, killed herself! They pieced it all together
in good faith to mean that she had fallen and crushed
her own throat and then dug her own fingernails deep
into the flesh of her neck, making a desperate attempt to
breathe.

"In my opinion the most probable cause of the injury
was external force received by falling on a sharp or hard
object, striking the right side of the throat against a chair
or table," this brief came from the very conscience of the
doctor who, looking at the pictures of the dead girl's throat,
decided that the wounds had been made "by grabbing at
the throat in desperation, trying to breathe, the way a
choking person acts."

Two other medical men pronounced this interpretation fantastic and unreasonable, against all common experience.

"Extremely unlikely that such wounds had been made by Miss Henderson's own hands," one doctor insisted.

"I have never seen people grab their throats when choking except in the movies," another added.

One of the doctors was a paid witness from another state, an authority on legal medicine. When it came out in the court that this man was accustomed to receive as much as $150 a day for his expert services, people sniffed and quite a few looked suspicious of well-paid opinion.

Rudy's fate could not remain undecided forever. It was time for him to take his life in his own hands. Like a film star he was compelled to make his personal appearance. His life might hang on a smile or a tear.

The sky was low and slate-colored the day Rudy went on the stand. There was a crowd throughout the courthouse and in the jury room people stood in the back. Green, red, and orange scarves, boys in checked woolen shirts, fur gloves, ear muffs, boots of red rubber tipped with rabbit fur, damp cheeks—in this winter gaiety the boy on the witness stand, still wearing the same tweed jacket, gray trousers, the same string tie, looked forlorn and orphaned.

Here he was at last, pale-eyed, soft-voiced: Rudy Peck.

"Now that it's gotten around to him, there isn't so much he can say after all. I don't see what's left except to repeat what's already been said," Parks whispered. "Poor devil. People are expecting so much from this appearance they are bound to be let down. He can't bring the girl back!"

Parks was anticipating, that quality in himself which could never be vanquished, that peculiar impatience which made him live through everything twice, in a double exposure.

"How would you describe him? I'm sure the reporters will choose *confident,* but they mean to be ironical, of that I'm certain. In a mess like this only a fool would appear

confident. . . . And what is there to say? Yes? What?"
Anita asked in a dispirited voice.

"I'm sure he can add something—"

"He could, *certainly!* But is this the place to add it?
He's got to be so careful. You must think of every word.
They trip you up on an adjective, these lawyers. You
could hardly tell the pure truth in any case, but you'd
need to think what they would make of it, how the truth,
even innocent truth, would be interpreted!"

"I begin to think you don't believe in the jury system,"
Parks said in a mocking tone.

"I'm just talking nonsense pure and simple!"

But Anita *was* less interested in Rudy's appearance on
the stand than she had expected to be. In her mind this
young man was so firmly placed his actual performance in
his own defense came as an anticlimax, and might even
disturb the cordial arrangement she had made of his
nature. Rudy's comradely gentleness, alert to the responses
of others to an exaggerated degree—this made it clear, she
decided, that he was only mildly ambitious, not truly
seeking to have power or to dominate. Beyond all he
seemed eager to arouse affectionate approval. Anita saw
in him a character loath to give pain, adaptable, fluid.
She sympathized, although these were not the qualities
she most admired.

"I suppose we've got that grim evening to go through
again," she whispered to Parks. "We'll get it all once
more, the dinner, the dance. . . . There have been so
many like it everywhere, except the end—"

"But the end after all!" Parks interrupted quickly.

"Oh, I think it was just as tragic as you do!" his companion said briskly, now looking at the jury. "They are embarrassed too and tense. . . . For him or for themselves? All of this is for them, they count for everything now. . . . Look, they are swearing him in! He's taking the oath!"

"That he is!" Parks said.

At first Rudy spoke almost inaudibly, his eyes imploring his lawyer, Mr. Brice. In a faltering voice he said he had been born in an Iowa town not far from this one, had gone to school there, been in the army, attended the University where he was studying economics.

Mr. Brice tenderly, his manner paternal, guiding, answered Rudy's fixed gaze with a great smile. He hesitated, waiting for the magic of his presence to do its work and Rudy at last took a deep breath, cleared his throat. Mr. Brice jumped in again, asked in a bright voice, as if he were not afraid for the whole world to hear, "Now, Rudy, did you know Betty Jane Henderson during her lifetime?"

Rudy looked astonished by the simplicity of this question and slowly replied, "Yes, sir."

"Speak up so that the jury can hear you," the judge said suddenly.

"Yes, sir, I'm sorry," Rudy said in a firmer, more normal voice. The judge nodded.

Mr. Brice began again. "You knew Betty Jane quite well, did you not? Had been engaged to her, given her your fraternity pin, and she accepted it?"

"Yes, sir."

"Now, Betty Jane received some injuries, did she not, Rudy?"

And there it came at last, after the conversations at the

water fountain, after the lingering about in the lobby day after day, after the bone-thin conversations with his parents, after the reporters, the twitches, the hopeful concentration, the exhibits passed out to the court, the dissected corpse itself—after all this endured with a sob, a blush, a twitch, for the first time there came over the young man's face a look of utter desolation, a sheet of ice.

"Yes . . ." he whispered.

"On this night you had returned to your rooming house at what time?"

"About midnight, thereabouts," Rudy replied, his voice returning.

"Why did you go there?"

"We thought we would have a nightcap, stay only ten or fifteen minutes."

Mr. Brice took off his glasses and rubbed the bridge of his nose. "Now, Rudy, will you tell the jury as accurately as you can what happened that evening after you went back to your room on Carson Street."

"Ah," Rudy said after a pause, "she was . . . standing in the middle of the room laughing. I poured out a drink first. . . . She didn't even have her coat off, because we only intended to stay such a few minutes. . . . We . . . ah . . . we embraced."

"Did Betty Jane return your embrace?" Mr. Brice asked boldly.

"Yes, she did."

"And then what happened?"

"Jokingly she placed her hands on my throat—"

"She placed *her* hands on *your* throat?"

"Yes, sir."

"And then what?"

"I said something to her, something about her hands being up too high. I said that was not the right way to choke a person, something like that as a joke. . . . Then I lightly put my hands on her throat. . . . Almost immediately she had a very strange expression on her face, very unusual. She looked in pain when I touched her throat . . . and then she moved away from me a little with this funny look on her face. . . ."

"Did you put both your hands on her throat in a real grasp?"

"No, I did not. Just my fingers very lightly."

"And all this time, Rudy, you were not holding Betty Jane tightly? Is that correct?"

"I was not holding her tightly," Rudy said in a clear voice.

"She could move away easily?"

"Yes, that's right."

"And then what did you do?"

"Then . . . We were standing there and she moved back . . . and then I went over to her and we began to dance, sort of to dance. I noticed she was moaning and gasping and I stared at her, wondering what was wrong. . . . She moaned and gasped and began to stagger a little bit. . . ."

"What did you do?"

"I don't know. I was paralyzed with confusion, seeing her suddenly like that."

"Did she speak?"

"No. Just moaning."

"Now, Rudy, how long was all this going on, the staggering and moaning?" Mr. Brice asked.

"I don't know. I think a very short time, maybe seconds, minutes, I don't know exactly."

During the questioning Rudy's parents sat with their heads down, their hands shading their eyes. Sometimes Rudy's glance would fall on their foreheads, fixing itself there while he spoke.

"To the best of your knowledge it was a very short time?"

"Yes."

"Well, Rudy, did you see Betty Jane Henderson make any attempt to relieve her pain at that time?"

At this point Rudy turned his head toward the jurors. Looking in the direction of these twelve people, his glance going from one to the other, he said, "Yes, I did."

Mr. Brice, rapid, but offhand: "Will you please describe these actions, these movements? Tell the jury about them just as accurately as you can, giving them the whole thing to the best of your knowledge."

Rudy began quietly to sob. A collection of tears in his voice prevented him from speaking immediately. After a moment he started, "Well, when this strange behavior came on I didn't know what to do. She moaned and gasped and I saw her put her hands on her throat. She seemed to be pulling at it or scratching at it rather, desperate movements. . . . She staggered and stumbled, taking a few steps about the room, moving toward the bed—"

"Now, Rudy, will you tell us again what you were doing at this time?" Mr. Brice said in a sad voice.

"Yes, sir. I suppose I was just staring at her. It was only

seconds, all so quick. It didn't sink in that she was in pain, choking. I didn't understand what was the matter."

"After she stumbled what happened?"

"She stumbled, by the bed . . . and then she fell, hitting upon the edge of a chair in the room . . . a straight-backed kitchen chair . . . with sharp knobs, which was in the room there. . . . She fell, gasping slightly and not saying a word, not a word. . . ."

"Could you tell what part of the chair she fell against?"

"Yes, it was against the sharp edge that she fell."

"Did Betty Jane move after that?"

"Yes, she tried to get up . . . was holding on the chair, on the edge after she had fallen and hit her neck. . . . To the best of my memory, at that moment she tried to get up and then she fell back again. . . . The next thing I clearly remember is being on the floor beside her. . . . I don't know how I got there. . . . I don't remember clearly what happened . . . it was all so fast and so confusing. I was stunned I think by the suddenness of it."

Breathlessly Rudy came to a stop. "Did you remember what you said just now when you made your first statement?"

"No, I couldn't remember then. What I have just told you was all in a jumble in my mind at first from the shock of the thing."

"How did you remember it?"

All of it had taken place very quickly, Rudy repeated. At the police station later, even in jail after he had been indicted, he felt quite confused about that December Friday evening, far from certain of the actual happenings in those terrible minutes. Only later had he uncovered it,

194

pieced it together by the help of drugs. With the court's permission after his arrest, he had voluntarily submitted himself to the local psychiatric hospital. There with the aid of relaxing drugs he had been able to recall the evening. He had recalled what he had just then described for the court.

And so his explanation was that he had placed his fingers lightly on Betty Jane Henderson's throat. This touch was without any sort of malicious intent but she had reacted painfully to it: extraordinarily the air supply had been cut off. Struggling to breathe, she dug her own fingernails into her neck thereby accounting for the external puncture wounds. Staggering, falling, she crushed her throat internally, causing the fractures when she fell against the edge of a chair.

Mr. Brice stroked his chin thoughtfully. "Now, Rudy, what were your feelings toward Betty Jane?"

"I was in love with her," Rudy answered immediately.

"Did she reciprocate your love, in your opinion?"

"I know she loved me," Rudy said proudly.

Mr. Garr objected to this answer as a "self-serving declaration."

"Self-serving declaration!" Parks whispered to Anita. "Amazing phrase. Make a very good title for a story!"

Mr. Brice rephrased the question. "Rudy, did Betty Jane often tell you she loved you?"

"Yes, many times."

"Was your fraternity pin returned by Betty Jane, or rather returned in the mail by her parents?"

"Yes, it was. In the summer."

"What did Betty Jane say to you about this?"

"She said she still considered herself engaged to me, but she could not keep the pin because of her parents' objections. The fact that she wasn't actually wearing the pin didn't change her affections, she said."

"Did Betty Jane state whether or not her parents were trying to prevent her from going with you, trying to change her affections?"

"Yes, she told me they didn't approve of her being pinned to me and she allowed them to send the pin back just to keep the peace."

"After the pin was returned you had dates with Betty Jane, did you not?"

"Yes, many times."

Mr. Brice did not appear the least fatigued with this line of questioning. Romantically, tenderly he paced the trail of love without stumbling, confirming these lovers with his audacious jaunts, his unsurprised heart and his recurrent sentiment.

"Rudy, on the night of December 12th, on that very night did you have the occasion to speak with her of your love? Will you please tell the jury about this?"

"Yes . . . we talked about these things that night. Yes, several times in fact during the evening I told her I loved her and she said that she loved me. We talked of our plans for the future. . . . After I graduated I hoped to get a job in the West, we both thought we'd like that. . . . California or Washington maybe. . . ."

Rudy daringly faced the jury as he said this. He went over it slowly and firmly, seizing this love which held his destiny, guided his stars, at least in the opinion of his lawyer. She loved me, she loved me, he was saying. Why had I cause to be jealous?

"Suppose she did love him?" Anita said. "What does it prove? This is a bore!"

Mr. Brice shot one more love dart. "Now, young man . . . did Betty Jane ever mention getting married before you finished school, just going ahead with it?"

A faint smile passed across Rudy's lips. "Yes, we would talk that way sometimes, think we'd just go on and take the plunge, but we didn't seriously plan it until I graduated."

Anita winced painfully before Rudy's declarations. They seemed to her quite the opposite of "self-serving." She did not believe a courtroom to be a felicitous setting for talk of love.

Mr. Brice suddenly shifted. "These statements you have made to the jury today are more detailed than those in your first statement, the statement taken on the night of the event here at the police station. Can you tell the jury why that is, why the two statements are not the same?"

Briskly Rudy replied, "Yes, I think I can explain. . . . I was in a state of shock that night. . . . I hardly knew what had happened, hardly knew what I was saying. . . . It was so sudden and so late at night . . . I was confused and did not accurately remember the evening until later."

"What were your feelings when Betty Jane asked another boy to her sorority dance?"

Rudy coughed. "I discussed it with her. I did not mind at all. We both thought it was the thing to do. I didn't want her to have any more trouble with her parents than

197

necessary and I knew they would be sure to hear if I attended the dance as her guest."

"It was agreed between you, then, that she should give an invitation to another escort?"

"Yes, sir."

"If she didn't think it wise to ask you to her dance, how did she feel free to accompany you to the dance your fraternity gave?"

Parks shook his head crossly as he awaited the answer.

"Her parents were not acquainted with people in my fraternity. It was quite otherwise in the case of the sorority."

Mr. Brice seemed well pleased. Now turning around, hardly looking at Rudy, but facing the jury he said with a ring, "Rudy, did you do anything to Betty Jane Henderson to injure her or to take her life?"

"No, sir, I did not!"

Mr. Garr, the prosecutor, rose up like a gray morning. He did not grow less dim, gray, and plain as the trial went on, but rather more so and to good effect representing the eternal reservation, the sober citizen at his tasks. Arms folded, rimless glasses shining, Mr. Garr looked a bit stiff and weary from these "explanations."

He led Rudy once more over the worn path of that December evening. "You were aware, I believe, that to take Miss Henderson to your room went contrary to University regulations?" he asked in a somewhat bored voice.

"Yes, I was."

"But you did return to your room around midnight,

nevertheless, in spite of the regulations? Is that correct?"

"That is correct."

"Now, Mr. Peck, did I understand you to say that you just barely placed your hands on Betty Jane Henderson's throat?" Mr. Garr's voice lifted in expectation at the end of his question, almost as if he believed his own being, his gray, guileless presence, the naked candor in his eyes, would bring forth a new, fresh, and unexpected answer.

"Yes, not even my whole hand, just my fingers," Rudy replied, his eyes upon the golden tip of a fountain pen in Mr. Garr's pocket. "That is correct, very lightly, with little or no pressure, sir . . . just demonstrating a silly game, as we had done before. No pressure . . . And then, then she suddenly looked strange and gasped, as I said. . . ."

"And then what?" Mr. Garr said, quietly staring.

"She stumbled. . . . She fell against the chair. . . ."

"Pardon, I meant and then what did you do?"

"I was stunned, petrified. . . . I didn't know what to do. . . . I thought it would pass, that she would be all right in a moment. . . . I can't remember what I did. I remember next being on the floor beside her, where she had fallen."

"You say she was gasping and moaning?" Mr. Garr continued, knitting his brows.

"Yes, sir."

"And while she was gasping and moaning and staggering about you did nothing?"

"I was amazed to see her like that. . . . It frightened me . . . such a short time, there wasn't time to do anything. . . ."

199

"You say the next thing you remember is being on the floor beside her. How long is your loss of memory?"

"I don't know. A few minutes, I suppose."

"Do you think you passed out, fainted?"

"I don't know."

Mr. Garr paused, his hand on his chin. "You don't know how long?" he asked finally, as if this lack of information were a pity.

"No, I don't know."

"So . . . When you were sitting on the floor beside Betty Jane Henderson, as you describe . . . when you came to on the floor beside her . . . what happened then?"

"I heard gasping, fainter now, and a sort of whistling sound. . . . I didn't know what it was. . . . I was terrified. . . . I touched her, spoke to her, called to her. . . . I was stunned. . . . At that time I saw a drop of blood in one nostril. . . ."

"Mmm . . . a drop of blood . . . What did you do?" Again Mr. Garr's voice surged up in wonder and in expectation of a new answer to the mystery.

"I didn't know what to do. I raised her as well as I could onto the bed, took off her coat and my own, trying to help her. . . . I did what I could, what occurred to me. . . . I felt her pulse, tried artificial respiration, but she didn't seem better and I was really frightened, had come to my senses after the shock. . . . I grabbed my coat and ran out of the house to get help just as fast as I could."

"To get help just as fast as you could?" Mr. Garr asked lightly.

200

"Yes."

"Or once you were out to get to the police station as fast as you could?"

"I thought that the best place to go at that hour."

"Did you seek the aid of any of the ten college boys who lived in the house on Carson Street?"

"No, I did not."

"Not at any time during the happening? Why not?"

"I was very much confused. They didn't seem to be the proper persons to call. Once I realized how serious it was I wanted to get professional help."

Mr. Garr took all this in, sighing and looking. He went on to later events in the case. "That night in the police station when you were being questioned one of the men on the force reports that you said, 'I must have done it. Who else could have? I was the only person there.' Now, is that man telling the truth when he reports those as your words in that place?"

"He may be. . . . I may have said that. . . . I don't know. . . . I was frighteened and numb."

Mr. Garr chewed on his lip. "Mr. Peck," he said easily. "Did you go to see Dr. Ashton last September?"

"Yes."

"Did you go to consult him about homicidal impulses toward the girl you were in love with and suicidal impulses toward yourself?"

Rudy cleared his throat, glanced about the room, his eyes weary, his face now faintly feverish. Hesitating, catching his breath, he nervously turned a ring on his finger. The courtroom waited, tense but mercilessly waited. Rudy's mother looked up at the judge, who was writing away on his pad; their glances met and she turned away quickly, looking toward the window. Even the reporters, all together, their ears alert, turned their worldly, unshockable faces to the witness, their expressions and lifted eyebrows wondering if he had an answer to that one.

Coughing again, Rudy said, "Yes, I went to see Dr. Ashton last September. Call it *consult* if you like. In my opinion I just wanted to talk these matters over with him in a scientific way. He had been my psychology teacher and I was very much interested in the subject. I wasn't worried about these impulses, not afraid. My attitude was something else. I was curious about them, curious about the probable origin, the general meaning. . . . Intellectually curious, I mean."

"You say you were not *worried* about impulses to kill the girl you were in love with!" the prosecutor put in.

"I don't know that *was* the impulse exactly! I can't remember precisely how I might have phrased it to him. When I say that I wasn't worried I mean that I knew these were psychological phenomena of the kind we had studied in class—"

"You were curious, then?"

"Yes, I was."

Mr. Garr lowered his gaze, dismissing the consultation with the psychologist with a baffled shrug. "All right then, Mr. Peck," he continued. "Now, did you tell Mrs. Finch that you had gone to Michigan to kill Betty Jane Henderson and hadn't been able to go through with it?"

Every head was turned to the witness box in spite of the drowsy heat. "No, sir! No, I did not!"

"You did not?" Mr. Garr said softly, amazed.

"No, I did not!"

"Did you *ever* talk to Mrs. Finch?"

"Of course, when we both worked at the restaurant and I saw her every day I'd speak to her, just as I did to everyone else. I am sure my conversations were entirely impersonal, had only to do with our work, whatever would normally come up in the kitchen!"

"So, you never spoke to her about Betty Jane Henderson?"

"I can't say I *never* spoke to her on that subject. The name may have been mentioned, I don't remember."

"But you did *not* tell Mrs. Finch that you went to Michigan in the summer to see Betty Jane? That you meant to kill her, but hadn't the nerve to go through with it?"

"I did not, sir!"

"You did not?" Mr. Garr repeated, still surprised rather than argumentative. "But Mrs. Finch testified under oath that you did so. Do you mean to tell the jury that she came here and told a deliberate lie?"

Rudy stared back grimly at the lawyer. "I can't say that it was a *deliberate* lie. . . . I have no idea why she came here and testified as she did. . . . I did not tell her what she says I did. . . . I'd say she was overworking her imagination!"

Mr. Garr looked at him sadly again, shook his head, and retired.

Before the session was over Mr. Brice returned to ask Rudy his final question. "Rudy," he said in a voice of touching seriousness, almost a prayerful one, "Rudy, did

you do anything to Betty Jane Henderson to injure her
or to take her life?"

"No, sir, I did not!"

"So there it is!" Anita said. She pulled on her black coat
with the Persian collar and straightened her hat, a black
toque decorated with a large silver pin. "I'm off! The
lawyers will sum up briefly and then it's left to the panel
of his peers!"

"Yes, destiny is turning the corner and will soon be
upon him," Parks said with a joking flourish. "It's hard to
realize everything's been said. Here it stands. There's no
more argument. It's all over! He's theirs," pointing to the
jury, "they own him."

"I feel as if they were getting ready to judge me too!"
Anita said. She and Parks stared at the fearful body of
twelve, who seemed, they decided, paler as the hour of
duty drew near. "They've been going home every night,
but now they'll stay here in the courthouse until the verdict is reached. And who knows what on earth they will
decide, even what they'll talk about, what aspects of the
thing." She studied the jurors faces as they waited for the
judge to call a recess. "Yes, that's that or will be very soon!"
she said, smiling wanly at Parks, who noticed her pale face
and the pink lips from which her vivid lipstick had worn
off. "I suppose I asked too much of him. Of course, I
don't know what will go with the jurors, but his testimony did not appeal to me somehow. I thought it was too
mushy. I feel sure he was capable of something more sub-
stantial."

"Many people I heard in the lobby thought it convincing, just the right thing," Parks said.

"You never know. We don't even know if it was the truth, any of it!"

"Now you're stretching it a bit, aren't you? But I was just thinking too how little we know, about him, about the case, about the girl. Right now, what are Rudy's thoughts? Perhaps under such a strain you really don't have secret thoughts as you would at another time. . . . I don't feel very hopeful somehow. . . . I heard one of the reporters say the jury looked like a tough one."

"How would the reporter know? What does a tough jury look like?" Anita demanded.

Parks threw up his hands. "Don't ask me. This fellow's been in on a lot of these trials, Iowa ones. He thinks he has an idea of how things are shaping up. And then there's the poll."

"The poll?"

"On the radio I heard the result of the reporters' poll among themselves. Split between manslaughter and second degree!"

"So . . . with either of those he'll get a number of years. It will ruin him. He'll just be a prisoner. Manslaughter is what? Accident, but with negligence, and second degree is murder but without premeditation. I'm never sure. . . ."

"I suppose we'll know in a day or so."

Anita and Parks left the courthouse, went down the steps for the last time. It was late in the afternoon and a strip of the sky was a brilliant red and purple with the dying sun blazing behind the snowy rooftops. It promised to be a clear, crisp winter evening.

They shook hands on the courthouse lawn, with a little embarrassment too, brought about by the prudence that had suddenly returned to them. Parks's fidelity to the court scene had put him behind in his studies, even though it had made him much in demand of an evening among his friends. He was glad the trial was over and yet he hated to resume, as the phrase went, "the even tenor of his ways."

"Beyond help now," he said vaguely.

"Good-by," Anita said. "This isn't my usual beat, court cases and all that. You mustn't think . . ." She smiled apologetically at Parks and went off to do her marketing, showing in the firmness of her step a decision to return seriously to her household duties.

The case would, after the last formalities, be in the hands of the jury, those twelve who had not only the truth to find, but to find each other since at this point each one was aware only of his own feelings and knew nothing of the inclinations of his fellow jurors.

"They will be obliged to stay out overnight, absolutely obliged to!" someone was saying. Other heads nodded, expressing agreement. It was generally felt that even if it were possible to arrive sooner at a verdict, even if these twelve strangers to each other should by extraordinary chance have the same opinions, they must suppress harmony and argue. A serious matter of this nature was not to be concluded quickly, one way or another. Some people looked at the jurors with envy, especially those who had pronounced emotions about the meaning of the case and others looked at them with simple curiosity, that same curiosity with which they viewed Rudy Peck.

Slipping away now, after the judge explained what the various verdicts would mean, the eight men and four women vanished into their mysterious sanctum, their isolation, their privileged and difficult debate. Blushing and solemnly the women clung together, while the men followed to begin their dialogue on what they had heard and seen in the courtroom during the last ten days. They were much in everyone's thoughts. Rudy, the lawyers, the public, the abandoned families waited for these absent ones to return.

"Do you think there'll be a split between the old and the young ones?" a young college boy wondered.

"May be more splits than that," a woman answered, grinning.

For the spectators the trial was over. It had been a long time beginning and was soon done with, some thought. These interested persons could return to their previous occupations, if any. They were no longer called upon to keep their faithful vigil in the early morning light before the closed doors of the courthouse. They were no longer asked to discover the heart's secrets, to answer the cries from the tomb. The "event," as Betty Jane's death was usually described for lack of another term without the verdict of the jury, the "event" has accomplished its history. It was already just another newspaper story, showing even now its inky dust, a yellow page in the Annals—of what, crime, tragedy, error, love? A happening not altogether clear in its details from the very beginning and now that the witnesses and testimony were finished "very confusing" according to the loitering voices in the lobby.

The orderly unfolding of evidence, the spectacle of the court, the drama of cross-examination, especially the presence—oh, so near!—of the accused himself, these could keep the nerves of a whole town on edge. As the jury left the courtroom the spectators had their last look at Rudy. Already their faces had an expression near indifference, acceptance of what must be, over and done with—the expressions one sees on the faces of a crowd at the end of a football game, vacant and bored even though just a few minutes before these same faces were alive with partisanship.

Shortly after lunchtime the next afternoon, Anita was joined by Harold March. He was a queer-looking figure today in a sealskin cap and a long coat lined with lamb's wool. "Have you come by sleigh?" Anita asked.

"I suppose this costume is a bit too Russian!" March exclaimed, tossing his cap on the sofa. "Well, you're very happy, aren't you?"

"Happy over what?"

Indolently, Anita straightened the pillows on the couch, thinking of March's pert face, his oddly snug and yet impetuous character which she accepted as "Southern." About this friend there was always a puzzle in her mind, intriguing, not unpleasant. It preceded March like a tune, his peculiar theme never fully stated. As a consequence of this sensation of not knowing all, Anita was very much afraid of boring him. When he arrived she did not expect him to linger long; when he departed she feared she had seen the last of him.

Today she did not like Harold March's eyes upon her. For several weeks now she had had the idea that he was criticizing her for going to the trial, imagining all sorts of absurd reasons, enjoying his own amusement at her scandalous devotion to the case, even seeing her perhaps as an empty soul wanting to be filled with horror.

"My God, don't tell me you haven't heard the news!" Harold exclaimed. "I call that self-persecution, the most dangerous kind of asceticism! You've been going to this thing nearly every morning for ten days and now seem entirely without interest in the outcome. Everyone else, people who wouldn't think of going to all the trouble you took, everyone else is fascinated. They've been hanging on the radio waiting for the verdict and now they have it!"

March was laughing at her and Anita found it difficult to keep her mind on what he was saying. She was thinking: He will never grow old. He's the sort that doesn't somehow.

"Well, what is the verdict? Tell me quickly! Of course I want to know and I was just thinking of turning on the radio but I was busy. Let's have it!" Anita said, taking a cigarette from the package March offered.

"You fool, he's been acquitted!"

"Acquitted? Entirely, altogether . . . You mean out of jail forever, not guilty!" Anita blinked her eyes so rapidly she might have been holding back tears.

"Yes, entirely acquitted! I don't think there are degrees for that! The thing's over. He's out of jail. The jury turned in a verdict of not guilty over an hour ago. I didn't hear it at the very first, someone stopped me on my way home, a perfect stranger, simply stopped, looked at me and said of all things, 'Exonerated!' I was so taken aback by that word I could hardly think what was meant."

"I am surprised, to put it mildly," Anita said. "Isn't everyone surprised, absolutely amazed in fact?"

"That I can't say!" Harold replied, speaking with great

enjoyment and amusement about this last part of the case. "I for one am surprised, but I expect it's a good thing. Everyone seems to like the boy, especially you!"

Anita gave him a scolding frown. "So he had no more to do with it than I had! Not at all concerned! Innocent bystander. Isn't that what the verdict means? . . . And all twelve of them agreed to that, all twelve! It's overwhelming. Yes, I can say I am profoundly surprised! . . . It separates the boy from the whole thing, doesn't it? He was not involved, in the real sense!"

"Don't be silly! You're exaggerating. The verdict means that they could not find him guilty. It doesn't mean that he had 'no more to do with it than I had' as you just said. That's going too far! They tried him for murder and didn't try you!"

"I am very much surprised!" Anita said again in a strained voice. "Who would have thought it? Simply acquitted!"

Again Anita found herself thinking of Harold March, briefly forgetting the trial and Rudy. Their friendship was an achievement of which she was proud—it was all the harder and more distinguished as an effort because of her feeling that she could not claim any sort of ownership. She was never even certain of her right to claim his attention. This was not due to any action on Harold's part who was unfailingly kind and lively in her presence but rather to her sensation that he was always thinking two things at once, not that one of these thoughts was hostile to her—no, it was not even concerned with her, nor with what they were saying.

Yes, she loved Harold March in a way she did not try

to define. Not as one loved a lover or a brother or a husband. No, one of those dim and yet splendid loves, something to be grateful for. This thin-necked March who always needed a haircut seemed to her to hold the key to mysterious regions, to inhabit some place between laughter and sorrow, some condition of being still unnamed, neither contentment nor misery, nor even acceptance. His snorting laugh like a cough—she never knew when to expect that. She was even pleased by something plebeian and a bit coarse about him, as though nature had begun this creation on a bigger, cruder, plainer scale and had then suddenly changed her mind.

"Acquitted entirely?" she repeated, her thoughts returning to the trial. "Are you sure, Harold? It would not be beyond you to trick me about this when the prisoner has just been given a life sentence!"

"Entirely acquitted, dear lady. Every word the truth. Even the redundant ones."

"What an odd decision for those people to make. Not at all what I imagined they were planning," Anita said, smiling.

"But I thought you were so eager to get the fellow off," March insisted. "You often made me feel just a little bit guilty that I wasn't out working up petitions for him or something. Your charity toward the boy made me feel a bit crass inside—I admit it now—because I couldn't always accept him quite so completely!"

"I don't believe a word about your feeling guilty—"

"But didn't you want him off?"

"Of course I wanted him to get off, certainly, naturally. But what I'm trying to say is that I didn't exactly think it would happen—at least not in such a thoroughgoing way. I would give anything to know how they analyzed the thing, how they argued it among them. . . . They must have argued, even these lenient judges! . . . I can't imagine how they arrived where they did, by what process. . . ."

March lit another cigarette. "That's a mystery. We will never know that, never get inside their minds. . . . One thing is clear at least. They certainly wanted him to get off and I think never even considered anything more serious than manslaughter. . . . You almost seem disappointed."

"Disappointed? No, that's not the right word," Anita said in a low voice. "It's perplexing more than anything. What mercifulness! I am convinced that if one asked those twelve people what sort of view they take of character they would all say in different ways that they take a more or less moral view of actions, and of course they do at least consciously—"

"Is mercy immoral?"

"I'm trying to say something else," Anita went on. "Nearly everyone professes to believe that people can be as good as they want to be, in a general way at the very least. We can be upright and morally acceptable if we want to make the effort. . . . But this verdict gives me the idea that perhaps this isn't believed any longer, not even by those who are certain they believe just that. I don't quite know how to explain the verdict otherwise. . . . It seems that even farmers, women, and typical citizens have all sorts of modern ideas without exactly knowing they have them. . . . You see, for that reason it

213

is so important, or at least *so interesting,* to know *why* they acquitted him. . . . I simply can't imagine *their* approach. I find it impossible to believe they went into all the psychological complexity of the thing, even in their secret thoughts. . . . In my view that was the kind of *doubt* which confused this issue . . . whether you could properly use *Guilt* and *Innocence* to describe it. . . ."

"Well, if they let him off as you seemed crazy for them to, I can't see honestly that it makes such a terrible difference to know just how they got to that point—"

"But it does make a difference! All the difference!" Anita's lips trembled and she did not look directly at March. "Of course I thought they'd want to be terribly tough on him. . . . Most people thought that, I believe. . . . It was hard to expect anything else from such respectable, typical people chosen from the community at large."

"You certainly misjudged them. That seems to be the long and short of the matter," March said gaily. "You thought you were a lot more sophisticated than they and you got roundly fooled—"

"It isn't *sophis-ti-cation!*" Anita argued, pronouncing the word slowly and scornfully.

"Ah, but yes it is!" March said dogmatically. "It rather frightens me, I confess! It is really unnerving to live in a world where *everyone,* just *anybody,* takes as complicated a view as the most clever people! When everyone sees things in all their paralyzing ambiguity—that's not so pleasant and comfortable after all! There's no one to uphold common sense!"

March hesitated, grinning at Anita, who now seemed

to have recovered her calm and was smiling back at him. "You funny old thing," he said tenderly. "I'm just beginning to see what a fantastic idea you had of this matter! You seem to think of this boy as having committed a sort of ritual murder, like the horde killing off the father in primitive times. For such an act there is no punishment that can be found in law books. The act exists on another level, a mythical, magical level. It has to be; it's the very nature of man to act in such a way and he cannot come to his own maturity in any other fashion."

"I don't think anything of the sort!" Anita said.

"No, perhaps you don't think poor Betty Jane Henderson was the father of the horde. . . . Then you seem to think in some way this boy had a sacred sort of psychic wound, sacred and blameless. The girl was meant to die, was compelled to let herself be murdered as a bird is compelled to sing. It was her destiny and it was the boy's destiny to kill her—"

"I don't think he killed her! That's the whole point," Anita said defensively.

"Oh, well, in that case justice is satisfied."

"But what did the jury think? There are so many unanswered problems."

"I haven't an idea on that."

March looked at his wrist watch. "Did I tell you I was going to Chicago for the week end?"

"No, I didn't know it! How nice for you. Are you going for any special reason?"

"Just for fun. The idea only came to me this morning and it seemed a good one." March looked at Anita with a sad and rather pained glance. "I'll be back on the six o'clock train Sunday, if anyone should call and need to know."

"Have a good time," Anita said, wondering at her feeling of embarrassment.

What, oh, what, did this friend want out of life? She was quite unable to imagine him at fifty. The course of nature did not seem to flow forward in its inexorable majesty in this instance.

When March had gone, Anita sat moodily smoking. She closed her eyes and sighed, thinking of Rudy, "What a lucky young man you are!" It amazed her to discover her own sudden aversion for Rudy Peck. Was it perhaps only that falling cadence one might expect, that steady diminishment of alarm and fascination as the night came to an end? It seemed to her to be more than this—in his sudden freedom the boy had been transformed into mediocrity, his history merely squalid and darkened with imponderables. What tremendous faith in him society had shown! Society had declared him innocent. Facing this idealistic decision, Anita acknowledged at last that she had not *quite* thought Rudy innocent—nothing so bald and clear as that. She had thought him innocently guilty. With "plain" innocence, his whole indictment was to be thought of as an outrageous error, a horrible, exhausting flight in the wrong direction. But guilty without desire, fundamentally without knowledge, guilty in this way he moved into a profoundly tragic light, took the stage and moved the audience to tears with his unbearable fate, his scarred, weeping, pitifully human mask.

Tired, she dozed briefly with a strange smile on her

216

lips. Later she was awakened with a jerk by the sharp, scalding sound of a cat outside her window.

"Scot free! Not guilty!" Doris informed her husband. Parks had understood the verdict could not be expected until five o'clock and so had spent the afternoon in the library.

"What do you mean?" he asked in a hurry, not quite ready to believe his first impression.

"What do I mean? Rudy's been acquitted! Innocent as a lamb."

"Acquitted, so . . . Really acquitted!"

"Not guilty," Doris said again. She looked brilliant today in a plaid skirt and red corduroy jacket, as fresh as a branch of holly, Mr. Emersen at the office had said. "I heard it all on the radio, all of them mingling together, Rudy, his mother, the lawyers, everyone. They were all very happy, crying, embracing. . . . It was something, take it from me! I felt like crying too."

"What a wonder!" Parks said, still standing near the door with his overcoat on. "How do you explain it? I hardly expected that amount of sympathy, did you?"

"I don't know what I expected. I suppose it was one of those emotional attacks . . . the jurors simply couldn't stand the thought of being responsible for the boy's punishment." Doris paused, pressed down a wing of hair on her forehead. "On the other hand, maybe they think he's innocent. They must!"

"So they think he's innocent," Parks said, brooding. "Yes, I suppose they do. . . . But in what way?"

"There's only one way to think it. He didn't kill the

217

girl, didn't do anything wrong, didn't plan or desire to harm her. *That* is innocence. What the verdict means."

"Mmm . . ." Parks said, taking off his coat and sitting down in the armchair. He had a grave air in the face of Rudy's acquittal. "I'm knocked out, pigeon! Taken completely by surprise! You see, I followed this thing very closely and I never imagined the jury could possibly come to such an agreement. . . . No one else dreamed of it either. It would be very interesting to know how they came to their decision."

"Aren't you satisfied? Or do you think they ought to award him damages to boot!"

"I'm satisfied! How could I be more so? Yes . . . Yes . . . But it's quite unexpected, nevertheless. . . ."

"Don't you think he's innocent?" Doris wanted to know. "Don't you agree with the jury?"

"I agree . . . in a way," Parks said cautiously. "Of course, in a certain way . . . I very much wanted him to get off, yes indeed. I'm delighted with the outcome, you know that. I believe it's all for the best, but that doesn't keep it from being surprising . . . especially to me, to someone who went through the whole thing."

Parks raised himself from the chair. "I think I'll fix a cocktail. Would you like one?" he said distantly, behaving with the reserve of a man in a difficult position.

"Martinis give me such a headache, but I suppose I'll try one with you."

Doris suddenly addressed her husband in a tart voice, "If you didn't honestly think the poor devil was innocent and still wanted him to get off—that's an attitude I can't understand, not that I myself am out for anyone's hide.

But to have one truth for oneself and want other people to be confused so that the truth won't have consequences . . . That's not for me . . . I think it's rotten!"

"Oh, nuts, Doris! I do think he's innocent! I was all for him, everyone knows that. But I still think there are many unanswered problems. . . . I would have predicted the jury would consider those problems more crucial than they apparently did!"

"No, no, no!" Doris said aggressively, her eyes flashing with the combat. "No, you're not telling the truth! You thought he was guilty as hell, but you wanted everyone to feel sorry for him because he was a poor boy whose father worked in a factory. . . . I know you, Joseph Parks, like a book! You wanted everyone to say, 'It's as clear as the nose on your face. . . . No wonder this boy killed the girl. He choked her because his father worked in a factory and hers didn't!' Of course, not *exactly* that. No one could be so foolish, but that is very nearly the way you looked at the case. Fantastic—"

"Don't be ridiculous! You're carried away," Parks said with renewed spirits. "But it was not a simple matter to judge. And there are many circumstantial factors which might have been expected to prejudice this group against Rudy. Nearly everything was out of order. First of all, as you said yourself, his taking the girl to his room, just that alone. Sometimes those things can matter enormously. A small indiscretion can make a crime seem more plausible."

"Well, he's completely free now! They took him at face value. That's what a lot of you seemed to want. . . . You got it." Doris laughed and bit into an apple. "Doesn't the State of Iowa look pretty impressive to you? Don't you

219

think these people must be extremely intelligent, very much aware, to arrive all by themselves at the very same idea you had—"

"I'm very much interested in the working of their minds . . ." Parks said, smiling too although dimly annoyed by Doris's remarks as one may be by a faint buzzing sound in the distance. "How little they revealed their intentions. You simply could not tell how they were responding to things. . . . They gave no indication, naturally. . . ." Parks sipped his Martini. "This is very good," he said, "especially with the onion in it."

"What went on in their minds? I imagine there was quite a bit of wind blowing about in that space just as there was in yours," Doris said cruelly. She finished her apple and tossed the core into the wastebasket. Out of the pocket of her red jacket she drew a long, thin cigarette holder, black and white. "How do you like this? Isn't it elegant? Only a dollar," she said gaily.

"I don't like it at all. Doesn't suit you," Parks replied indifferently.

"Oh, well, you know these things get misplaced somehow and you never use them more than a couple of times, like cigarette lighters. . . ."

"I think I shall telephone my friend," Parks said abruptly. "You know, that little Mrs. Mitchell I mentioned to you . . . the woman I often saw at the trial. . . . I wonder if she has heard about the verdict?"

"Of course she's heard about it," Doris said, puffing grandly on her cigarette holder. "I hope this is a virtuous attachment, this little Mrs. Mitchell you met at the trial."

"I'm afraid it is," Parks said gallantly as he went out into the hall.

Doris sat down on the bed, resting her head against the wall. On her face there came an expression of sly pride and amusement mingling with a sort of slumping contentment, like a puppy before the fire gratefully remembering the prompt bone, the playful slap.

That afternoon Mr. Emersen had put his hand on her breast. There was definitely a seediness about Mr. Emersen, Doris had discovered, a dryness and withering that crackled through his pipe-smoking serenity—his jauntiness and sportiness was as brittle as a match stick—yes, that was all true. But he was rather interesting, if not entirely enjoyable somehow—his impudent eyes were strangely distinguished and his vanity was such that she could not help feeling at least a little bit honored if he who loved himself so much also chose her as a friend, a runner-up in his affections.

Still I was very much annoyed, *honestly* annoyed, Doris was now saying to herself, remembering Mr. Emersen's sudden hand. I didn't appreciate the compliment, no indeed! I wasn't flattered, simply bored and irritated. And what is worse—I'll never feel comfortable with that stupid Emersen again. I shall have to quit my job, that's all there is to it. I can't possibly face him again on Monday. It will look as if I didn't mind at all and he is clever enough to know that any girl would notice what he did and has given quite a bit of thought to it since!

Doris was very happy to learn that these were her true feelings. She cocked her head forward to catch Joseph's conversation on the telephone. Through her mind as she half listened to her husband there passed the final image of Rudy Peck as she had imagined him from the radio broadcast. There he was for the last time, speeding away, farewell, weeping, shaking hands, waving, and then off with his little satchel of toilet articles used in prison! Sad, sad escape, Doris whispered, perplexed by her own thoughts.

She felt sorry for Rudy more than ever now. His freedom so fervently hoped for, life in the open again, a crash of riches!

"But no one feels the same about the friend who has won a lottery!" Doris observed, looking at her fingernails which were as smoothly, thickly red as fresh tulips. "We are now free to ask if we are satisfied, easy in our communal soul." Poor, poor Rudy! Anarchy left everyone ill, chewing upon the sour and bitter leaves in the bottom of the cup.

On the telephone Parks was saying, "Do you suppose the jury knew something we don't know? . . . You hardly think that possible? . . . But, what I can't figure out is the very simplicity of the verdict, it almost looks fishy. . . . Don't mistake me! . . . No, no, I don't mean the simplicity of the case, but the baffling finality of the verdict. . . . How awful it would be if the whole thing, the not-guilty, if this was merely a childish reaction on the jury's part. . . . Sentimentality . . . A way of showing they disapproved of the girl for *leading him on.* . . . Maybe they thought *she* shouldn't have allowed herself to be taken to the rooming house, no decent girl and all that rot. . . . I heard, you remember, people speculating

222

in those terms. . . . It is not just to use the double standard in that way. . . . Women . . ."

Betty Jane Henderson, delicate wrists and ankles, blue eyes, fair beauty scented with Eau de Cologne, sparkling gay and warm and within the reach of all like a rhinestone, her lips parted in a dazzling, white smile—*adieu!*

Doris put another cigarette in her black-and-white holder. A single cool tear clung pleasantly to her eyelashes.